The SEVENTH WISH

Also by Kate Messner

The SEVENTH WISH

Kate Messner

BLOOMSBURY

NEW YORK LONDON OXFORD NEW DELHI SYDNEY

First published in the United States of America in June 2016
by Bloomsbury Children's Books
www.bloomsbury.com

Bloomsbury is a registered trademark of Bloomsbury Publishing Plc

For information about permission to reproduce selections from this book, write to
Permissions, Bloomsbury Children's Books, 1385 Broadway, New York, New York 10018
Bloomsbury books may be purchased for business or promotional use. For information
on bulk purchases please contact Macmillan Corporate and Premium Sales Department at
specialmarkets@macmillan.com

Library of Congress Cataloging-in-Publication Data
Names: Messner, Kate, author.
Title: The seventh wish / by Kate Messner.
Description: New York : Bloomsbury, [2016]
Summary: Charlie feels like she's always coming in last. From her mom's new job to her sister's
life away at college, everything else always seems to be more important than Charlie's upcoming
dance competition or science project. Unsure of how to get her family's attention, Charlie comes
across the surprise of her life one day while ice-fishing . . . in the form of a floppy, scaly fish
offering to grant her a wish in exchange for its freedom.
Identifiers: LCCN 2015036430
ISBN 978-1-61963-376-6 (hardcover) • ISBN 978-1-61963-377-3 (e-book)
Subjects: | CYAC: Magic—Fiction. | Wishes—Fiction. | Family life—Fiction. |
Schools—Fiction. | BISAC: JUVENILE FICTION / Family / Siblings. |
JUVENILE FICTION / Fantasy & Magic. | JUVENILE FICTION / School & Education. |
Classification: LCC PZ7.M5615 Sh 2016 | DDC [Fic]—dc23
LC record available at http://lccn.loc.gov/2015036430

Book design by Colleen Andrews
Typeset by Newgen Knowledge Works (P) Ltd, Chennai, India
Printed and bound in the U.S.A. by Berryville Graphics, Berryville Virginia
4 6 8 10 9 7 5

All papers used by Bloomsbury Publishing, Inc., are natural, recyclable products
made from wood grown in well-managed forests. The manufacturing processes
conform to the environmental regulations of the country of origin.

For Linda, in admiration and friendship.
Long live the Mocha Latte Writers' Group.

The
SEVENTH
WISH

Chapter 1

New Ice

I've only seen the ice flowers once.

It was winter vacation when I was six and Abby was twelve. She came flying into my bedroom in her green-flannel pajamas. "Charlie, wake up! You have to come see before they're gone!"

We threw on coats, stuffed our bare feet and pajama bottoms into snow boots, and raced outside, down the street to the little rocky beach that leads to the lake. The rocks that sloped down to the ice were slippery, but Abby held tight to my hand. When their jagged edges gave way to smooth, flat ice, she let go and knelt down to stare at a little patch of snow over the blackness.

Only it wasn't snow. The night before had been clear and cold and full of frigid stars. It looked as if they'd fallen from the sky and turned to crystal in the morning light. A whole field of them stretched over the ice from our shore to the island way, way out.

Ice flowers.

"They're beautiful!" I thought they must be magic. Abby said she thought so too—and a morning that started with flowers of frost painting the lake could only turn into a magical day.

We ran back to the house, into a sweet maple-pancake kitchen, and told Mom all about the flowers and the maybe-magic. She smiled like she had a secret, and before we thought to ask where Daddy was, he walked through the door with Denver in his arms. We'd known we were getting a yellow Lab puppy—just not that very day.

When we took Denver outside to play later, the sun had melted the ice flowers' beautiful edges and turned them to regular frost. But for a few short hours, they'd decorated the lake in Jack-Frost magic for Denver and for us.

Now, every year on the first super-cold morning of winter, I go to Abby's room and bounce on her bed until she gets up and comes outside with me to look. Sometimes we find the lake churning with freezing waves that splash icicles onto the rocks. Sometimes it sits under a quiet blanket of ice fog, swirling in breezes we can't even feel. Sometimes it's frozen solid, black as ice can be.

But the ice flowers have only come once.

I've had a feeling this vacation week, though. They're bound to come again. And why not today?

It's a new year, with confetti stuck in the living room carpet from our celebration last night and a glossy new calendar on the fridge. On that calendar is a circled date—January 28—when I'm getting my solo dress for Irish dance.

It was a Christmas present from Mom and Dad—a note card that read "This certificate entitles the bearer to one solo dress for Irish dance (up to $300)." That might sound like a lot for one dress, but the truth is, it's barely going to cover the most basic one you can get. Fancier solo dresses cost more than a thousand dollars because they're covered in Swarovski crystals that catch the light and sparkle when you dance. Three hundred dollars isn't enough for crystals, but the dress will still be better than the plaid-skirt-white-shirt dance school uniform I have now.

New year. New calendar. New dress.

And a new record low temperature, according to the TV weatherman who gave the forecast wearing a New Year's party hat last night. It was supposed to get down to minus twenty-two.

Our furnace growled and moaned about that all night, and even though I know the wood floor will be cold on my feet, I jump out of bed because maybe this will be the morning the ice flowers come again. If they do, I don't want us to miss them.

I run down the hall to Abby's room, knock on her door, then burst in and pounce on her bed. "Abby, get up! We have to check for ice flowers!" I bounce on my knees and wait for her to sit up and whomp me with her pillow like she does sometimes.

Abby pulls the pillow over her head. "Charlie, it's like seven o'clock. Leave me alone."

Her voice is hoarse and scratchy, like maybe she's getting sick. But I can't believe she'd miss the ice flowers. "Ab?" I try to lift the pillow, but she pulls it tighter around her ears. "Come on . . . it'll only take a few minutes and then you can go back to bed."

"Go. Away."

"Fine. I'll go look myself." I leave her room and pull the door shut, harder than I need to.

When Abby left for college in August, I cried and cried. No matter how many times Dad reminded me that we could video chat, that she'd be home to visit, I knew it wouldn't be the same. And I was right. She texted a lot and sent pictures of campus the first couple of weeks, but after that, she was too busy with classes. Even though Abby's home for break now, she still feels far away, all sleepy and moody unless she's getting ready to go out with her friends. She didn't spend New Year's with us, even though Mom made tacos and brownie sundaes. It hardly feels like I got my sister back at all.

But I'm not going to let Abby's bad mood ruin the magic, if it's there. I rush to the kitchen door and put on my winter stuff. Mom and Dad are drinking coffee at the table. Dad lowers his newspaper and eyes my boots-with-pajama-pants outfit. "Where are you going, Charlie?" he asks at the same time Mom says, "Stay off that ice, Charlotte Anne."

She looks out the window, down the street toward the lake. "It's only had one night to freeze. That's not enough."

"I know. I just want to look."

Mom nods and goes back to the sports section, and I step outside. I have to catch my breath because even though the sun is bright, the blue-sky air is so cold it bites at my face. I can feel the inside of my nose freezing when I take a breath.

My boots crunch on the little bit of snow left on the sidewalk from last week's storm. It looks like there are patches of snow out on the lake too. But that can't be. It didn't snow a flake last night. I run until I get to the icy rocks, and then I slow down. I can already see them.

The ice flowers are back. They sprouted overnight, growing layer by icy layer while we slept under warm blankets in the dark.

They are just as magical as before.

I slide my foot out onto the lake's dark, frozen surface and test the ice with a little of my weight. My heart flutters in my chest. I've been a total chicken on the ice ever since I saw one of those cold-water-rescue shows on TV when I was seven. But I remind myself that the water's barely up to my knees here. Even if the ice cracked and I fell through, the worst thing that could happen is that I'd end up with really cold shins.

I take another step. The ice is solid enough to hold me—at least three or four inches, I can tell—so I slide out to the first silent patch of white and kneel down for a closer look.

I crouch low, the way Abby did all those years ago, to see more closely. Each perfect petal is like a feather cast in ice. I take a cold breath, and the air chills my insides. When I let it out, a gentle warm breeze, the flower crumbles to nothing. A smudge of once-was-magic left on a smooth, dark pane of glass.

"You check that ice with an auger?" The voice startles me, and I turn to see Drew's nana, Mrs. McNeill, standing at the shore in a snowmobile suit. Drew's next to her in snow pants and a jacket, holding a stick. Drew's been holding some stick or other since I met him in first grade. First it was always a pretend gun or a sword, and then it was a defense against grizzly bears and moun- tain lions (which don't live here, but Drew believes in being prepared anyway). Today, it looks like it's just an ice poker.

I stand up and brush flower-dust off my knees. "I don't have an auger, but it looks about three or four inches thick," I call, hoping Mrs. McNeill won't tell Mom. "The water's not deep here, if you want to come out."

Mrs. McNeill and Drew shuffle their way out to where I am. Mrs. McNeill looks down at the ice flowers. "Well, isn't that something." She squats low, just like I did, and breathes one away as if it's made of nothing at all. "These won't last long under the sun," she says, and sighs.

That makes me want to be careful where I breathe, where I step, so they'll last a little longer.

"You don't see these often around here," Mrs. McNeill says as she stands up. "They happen more up in the Arctic where—"

"Feels like the Arctic here," Drew says, wiping his nose on his coat sleeve.

"Gross," I say.

"It's not gross." He makes a face at me, then lifts his sleeve to inspect the shiny smear. "Did you know your nose and sinuses make a liter of snot every day?"

"Again. Gross." I shake my head, but I laugh. Drew is an expert on disgusting things. It was his idea to include scat samples in our animal tracking science fair project last May, which earned us ten points extra credit and me the nickname "Pooper Scooper" for the rest of the year.

"As I was saying," Mrs. McNeill goes on, and Drew rolls his eyes. She's a retired science teacher who takes care of Drew when his parents are working, which is pretty much always. Drew gets a lot of science lessons. "This pattern of frost formation is an Arctic phenomenon. When the air is very cold and ice forms quickly over warmer water, then . . ."

She keeps going a while, but I tune out. I blow puffs of steam into the frigid air and watch the clouds of breath fade away until Mrs. McNeill nudges me and says, "Think you could pass a test on that now?"

"I wasn't totally listening," I admit. "I guess I didn't want the science to wreck the magic."

"Science *is* a kind of magic," she says.

I nod. But I want beautiful, impossible-to-explain, ice-flower magic like the day we got Denver. Maybe I'll be able to find a perfect solo dress on sale to fit my budget.

"You oughta come fishing with us later," Drew says.

"Tomorrow," his nana corrects. "We need one more good cold night before it'll be safe to go out where the fish are. We'd love to have you come along, Charlie. We could use another fishing buddy." They used to fish with Drew's grandpa before he died three years ago.

"I don't ice fish," I say. The truth is, I love fishing in summer, but I don't do anything on ice that's covering water more than a couple feet deep. I'm not fearless like Abby. She and Mom and Dad always try to get me to go skating with them once the ice is thick and safe, but in my opinion, there's no such thing. Some poor dumb person who thinks it's thick enough falls through every year because it isn't. "Thanks, though."

"Aw, come on," Drew says. "We're entering the Make-a-Wish Derby. It raises money to send kids with cancer to Disney World and stuff. They got a grand prize of a thousand bucks for the biggest perch."

"Really?" When I think of wishes, all I can see is a solo dress covered in sparkling crystals.

"Yeah. And if we don't catch the biggest one, we can still sell 'em to Billy's Tavern, right, Nana?"

Mrs. McNeill nods. "Couple dollars a pound is all, but you have a good day and they add up."

I think about that. Maybe they wouldn't add up to enough for a super-sparkly dress, but even money for a few more crystals would help. "How far do you go out?"

"We stay pretty close these first few days," Mrs. McNeill says. "The perch like new ice."

"So do I." I kneel down to look at another frozen-lace flower.

Drew and his nana head back toward their house, but Mrs. McNeill turns back. "Don't go out any farther, Charlie. Just because that ice is pretty doesn't mean it's making you any promises. It needs another night to freeze. Let winter work its magic."

"Don't worry." I stand up and head toward shore too, listening to them argue as they walk.

"Can't we go out this afternoon?" Drew says.

"Tomorrow."

"What about tonight if it's real cold after supper?"

"Tomorrow."

"I wish the ice would hurry up."

"Wish all you want. Wishing doesn't make a thing so."

Maybe not, I think, but ice flowers do. They made our morning sparkle on the day we got Denver. Now, finally, they're back. And I'm ready for some more magic.

When I get home, I step into the kitchen and kick off my boots. Mom and Dad are arguing with Abby upstairs, but the kitchen is warm and there's cinnamon toast left on a plate. Denver's under the table, waiting for crumbs. I bite into a piece, then poke at the sugar crystals with my finger. I imagine them out on the ice, glimmering in the morning sun, then sparkling on a dress while I dance, arms at my sides, knees high.

Maybe ice fishing is a good idea after all.

Chapter 2

The Littlest Catch

"I'm thinking of a word," I tell Mom and Dad at breakfast the next morning.

Dad pushes his bagel into the toaster and looks up at the ceiling. "Vendetta?"

"Marigold," Mom says from the closet, where she's pulling out snowshoes.

"Dad wins. It was telegram."

"Ha!" Dad high-fives me on his way to get the peanut butter from the cupboard.

"Humph." Mom sets two pairs of snowshoes on the bench by the door. "How do you figure?"

"Because you could send a telegram about a vendetta, obviously," Dad says. "Nobody sends telegrams about marigolds."

"I hate this game," Mom says, laughing. The game is

totally stupid, but it's a family tradition. When I was five and Abby was eleven, we used to play the guess-what-number-I'm-thinking game. She'd tell me she was thinking of a number between one and a hundred. I'd guess five; she'd tell me if it was higher or lower, and I'd keep guessing until I figured it out. I thought it was the coolest thing ever—everything Abby did was cool—so I started bugging Mom and Dad to guess numbers. One day, I said I was thinking of a word, and everybody should guess what it was. Mom and Dad each guessed a few times before they explained there were too many words to play the game that way. But I loved the word game, so we decided everybody could guess once and whoever was closest to the word would win. After that, the word game just stuck around.

Abby even played with us from college this fall, via group text.

Abby: I'm thinking of a word.

Mom: I hope the word is study. ☺ Don't you have a test Friday?

Charlie: Diligent.

Abby: Oohhh, fancy guess.

Charlie: Vocab word.

Dad: THE WORD IS MARSHMALLOW.

Abby: Stop shouting, Dad. You're all wrong. It was jeggings. Mom wins because jeggings are comfortable study attire.

Dad tried to argue—still shouting because he doesn't know how to turn off the caps lock on his phone—that if you wear jeggings, you can eat lots of marshmallows because they're elastic. Mom said that was a stretch, and then she was all proud of her pun. (Get it? Elastic . . . a *stretch*?)

Sometimes, it's easy to decide who wins. Like if the word is dangerous, and Dad guesses dishwasher and Mom guesses mushroom, then she totally wins because of poisonous mushrooms. But it can get tricky. Once Mom and Dad argued for ten minutes over which word was closer to sunflower—flashlight or rebellious. (Flashlight won. Because of yellowy brightness.) Abby's always been the best at making a case for her guesses, but she's sleeping late again, so Dad wins the vendetta-marigold-telegram argument today.

"We're going snowshoeing in the park," Mom says, pulling snow pants from the shelf. Dad's an English teacher, and she's a part-time school nurse, so they have the whole winter break off too. "Want to come?"

"Actually, Mrs. McNeill invited me ice fishing with her and Drew."

Dad raises an eyebrow. "Wouldn't that involve going out on the ice? Last year, we couldn't even get you out skating once."

"I know. But she says we won't need to go out far. I think I'd like to try."

Mom goes to the window and glances at the thermometer. "Ten below." She makes a face as if she's calculating how much ice could have formed over a night that cold. "Okay. We'll see you back here for lunch."

"Should I ask Abby if she wants to come?"

Mom's eyes dart to the stairs and then to Dad, who grimaces and shakes his head. They've had a lot of serious kitchen-table conversations with Abby since her first semester grades showed up during vacation. I guess the grades weren't very good.

"I don't think Abby's quite ready to face the world this morning," Mom says. "Don't forget your phone. And dress warmly or you'll freeze to death."

Two sweaters, one puffy winter coat, two scarves, one pair of snow pants, one hat with ear flaps, and one pair of thick mittens later, I'm waddling across the yard to the McNeills' house. I feel like that snowsuit kid who couldn't move in the movie *A Christmas Story*, but it's too cold to be wearing anything less. The sun's out, though, so hopefully it'll warm up to zero soon.

Mrs. McNeill practically lives with Drew and his parents during fishing season. She and Drew are already out in his yard, getting fishing stuff ready. Drew tears open a package of Pop-Tarts and offers me one.

"What kind is it?" I ask.

"Strawberry. Duh."

"Thanks." When you've been friends as long as Drew and I have, you have a lot of conversations about which Pop-Tarts are the best (strawberry with frosting) and which are just gross (pumpkin, which has no business being anything but jack-o'-lanterns or pie).

"Hey, do you know what to do if you ever get buried in an avalanche?" Drew says through a mouth full of Pop-Tart.

"Nope," I say. Drew's nana gave him *The Worst-Case Scenario Handbook* a couple of years ago, and he's read it cover to cover, fifteen times. Sharing techniques for surviving unlikely catastrophes is his favorite thing in the world besides fishing. "What should I do?"

"Spit in the snow," Drew says, and spits on the snowy yard.

"How's that going to help?"

"You make a little air pocket and spit, and then gravity will tell you which way is up and which way is down. Then you aim up and dig like crazy."

"Good to know." I wonder if I'm in for a whole day of survival training. "Hey, is Rachael coming fishing with us?" Drew's older sister is a senior in high school and the coolest person I know other than Abby. Rachael's the one who got me into Irish dancing, only she's way better at it. She was seventeenth in North America last year.

"Nah," Drew says through a bite of Pop-Tart. "She's got some dumb *feece* to go to."

"It's *feis*." I pronounce it the right way—*fesh*—even though Drew already knows that's what the Irish dance competitions are called. The plural is *feiseanna* (fesh-ee-AH-nuh). Drew always calls them *feces* instead. It drives Rachael nuts. "Where is this one?"

"Rochester, I think."

Part of me wishes I could be there to watch, but then I remember that ice fishing is going to help me pay for the solo dress for my own feis in Montreal later this month.

"Got decent tread on those boots?" Mrs. McNeill asks me, and I hold up a foot to show her.

"Nope," she says, and hands me a pair of ice cleats. "Wrap these around the bottom of your boots or you'll be slipping all over the place."

I do that while she and Drew load poles, augers, and bait buckets onto the sled. Then we head out onto the lake. Right by shore, there's a hole in the ice with a pile of shavings around it. "Were you out already?" I ask.

Mrs. McNeill nods and kicks at the circle of snow. "Drilled a hole to check the thickness. We have a good six inches, so we're all set." She leads us away from shore onto the clearest black ice.

The ice flowers are still here, but they're flat and muffled today, like wildflowers someone pressed in a book. They crunch under my feet as we head toward a point of land sticking out from shore.

I'm taking careful steps, one foot in front of the other, and managing to convince myself this is safe. But when we're halfway out to the point, the ice lets out a booming-loud, timpani-drum thump. I've heard muted ice sounds from shore before, but this is *loud*. I jump about a mile and look at Mrs. McNeill. "Is it breaking up?"

"I know how to survive being stranded on an iceberg," Drew says.

"I'm *so* hoping we don't need that information right now," I tell him.

Mrs. McNeill gives me a reassuring smile and shakes her head. "The ice is fine, my dear. You're simply hearing air bubbles working themselves up through the fissures now that the sun's up. Listen . . ." She pauses, and the ice booms again, like thunder out by the island a mile offshore. Then it makes a weird, video-game sound. *Gurgle-twang-zzzing!* "That's the ice talking, letting us know it's settling in for a good, long winter of fishing."

I keep going. But my heart's still pumping fast, and my legs feel wobbly, even with the cleats. If this ice really means to be reassuring, it ought to talk in something other than loud, scary growls and space invader weapon sounds. Right now, I'm hearing less "We're going to have a good winter" and more "I'm going to swallow you whole."

Not far from the point, Mrs. McNeill pulls the sled to a stop and looks around. "You think this is about where we were in the boat?" she asks Drew.

"Pretty close." Drew turns to me. "There's a ledge around here where the perch like to feed. We were pulling 'em in like crazy back in August."

They start unloading gear from the sled. I pick up an insulated bucket and can feel the bait sloshing around inside. "Are these minnows?"

"Yep. They're always better than lures when you can get 'em." Mrs. McNeill pulls a power auger from the sled and turns to Drew. "Shall we let Charlie give this a try?"

"Sure, as long as I get to drill my own," he says.

"I don't know how to use that," I say. The auger has a pull cord like the outboard motor on the McNeills' boat, and I couldn't pull hard enough to get that started last summer.

But Mrs. McNeill leans over to show me. "Piece of cake," she says. "Pull the rip cord." I do that, and the motor starts humming. "Great!" She points to a trigger thing on the auger's handle. "Now give it some gas to make the blades turn, and we're in business." She guides the auger to a spot on the ice and holds it with me, pressing down while the blades whirl into the ice. In a few seconds, there's a hole about six inches wide and a sparkling circle of ice shavings all around it. "Perfect!"

She hands the auger to Drew, who makes his own hole about ten feet farther out. Then he pulls three short fishing poles from the sled and hands one to me. It's only a couple feet long, way smaller than the poles we use in summer.

I take off my mittens, fish out a minnow, and bait the hook. My bare hands burn with the cold. Once they're mittened up again, Mrs. McNeill gives me a quick ice fishing lesson.

"You want to drop your bait maybe two or three feet down," she says, "and be sure to give the pole a good tug when you feel a bite. They can get away quick." She puts the lid on the bait bucket and slides it over so I can use it as a stool. "One more thing before you fish . . ." She reaches under her scarf, pulls out a four-leaf clover charm on a chain, and holds it up. "May the luck of the ice spirits be with you."

"That doesn't sound like science," I say.

She smiles and tucks the charm back under her layers of wool. "Drew's grandfather gave it to me when we got engaged years and years ago. He said it was a good luck charm, and I decided I'd believe that. It hasn't always worked for me, but I've learned that you take your magic where you can get it. Especially when you're waiting on fish to bite." She heads farther out on the ice, a little past Drew, to drill another hole, and I drop my line down under the ice to wait.

There's a lot of waiting in ice fishing, and now that I'm not moving, it feels colder, even with the sunshine. The air is still biting, and my fingers never warmed up inside my mittens. I hold my pole with one hand and lift the other to my mouth to blow some heat onto them. Twenty minutes go by in silence, except for the ice groaning and thumping.

Finally, Mrs. McNeill stands up. "Got one!" she hollers, and reels in a perch.

Drew stands up to see. "Ain't big enough to bother with in the derby, but Billy'll take it."

"*Isn't*," Mrs. McNeill says. Drew totally knows better, but he loves the cowboys in old Western movies and knows it drives his nana crazy when he talks like them.

Mrs. McNeill pops the lid off her bucket, drops the fish inside, covers it, and sits down. Almost right away, she has another fish, and then Drew stands up. "I got one too!"

I keep waiting for a tug on my line. Drew pulls in three more fish, and Mrs. McNeill catches a bigger one. "This fella's got a chance, don't you think?" She holds it up, and Drew nods. She puts it in the bucket and calls to me. "Charlie, I bet you're in too shallow. Why don't you come out where it's a little deeper, and we'll set you up with a new hole?"

I shake my head. "I like this hole." That's because I'm pretty sure the water underneath it isn't over my head.

Another half hour goes by. Drew and Mrs. McNeill have at least twenty fish between them. I haven't even had a bite yet, but the thought of going out any farther on this ice makes my knees wobble. My hands are freezing, and my nose is running, and I can't remember why this seemed like a good idea. There's not much use fishing when you're afraid to go where the fish are.

Apparently, ice flowers don't have enough magic to turn me into a fisherman.

Fisherwoman.

Whatever. It's not going to happen.

"Woo-hoo!" Drew starts reeling in another one, and I'm about to give up when I feel the tiniest pull.

"Oh!" I stand up and give a tug, and at first I think the fish got away because it feels like I'm reeling in a whole lot of nothing. But when the line comes up, there's a tiny perch flopping on the end. It's not much bigger than the minnow I used as bait, but at least it's something.

"She's got one!" Mrs. McNeill shouts from across the ice.

Drew turns and looks. "You call that a fish?" He snorts out a laugh.

I ease my miniscule catch off the hook. "Should I let it go?"

"Nah, Billy'll take it. Put it in the . . . whoa!" Drew's pole almost jumps out of his hand. He turns around and starts reeling again. Mrs. McNeill's got another bite too. I stand up, holding the fish in one hand, and pull the lid off the bucket with the other.

"Please," someone says.

And I freeze. Because it's not Mrs. McNeill and it's not Drew. And it's not the stupid growly ice talking this time either. This voice is quiet and low-pitched and raspy.

"Please," it says again.

I look at the fish in my hand. It's a skinny thing, only about five inches long, black-and-green striped with orange on its fins. But instead of plain, glassy-black eyes like the other perch I've seen, this fish has bright-green eyes that almost glow. Like emeralds. Crystals. And this fish is looking right at me.

"Release me," the raspy voice says, and I swear I see the fish's mouth moving a tiny bit, as if it's gasping for breath.

But it can't be. Fish breathe through gills. That was one of Mrs. McNeill's lakeside science lectures last summer. And the bigger issue here is not how a fish breathes but that this one is talking. To me.

I look up at Mrs. McNeill and Drew, rebaiting their hooks. "Did you guys hear that?"

"Hear what?" Mrs. McNeill tips her head. The ice lets out a gurgle. "Oh, honey," she says, "those sounds aren't going to hurt you. I wish you'd come out a bit. You'd have more luck."

"I got another one!" Drew shouts. "Come on . . . be the big one!" He starts reeling again.

I stare down at the fish in my hand.

"Release me," the raspy voice says again, "and I will grant you a wish."

Chapter 3

The First Wish

"A wish?" I say.

"What?" Drew calls from his hole.

"Nothing." I stare at the fish in my hand. It's not talking anymore. It's flopping. Struggling. Did I imagine it?

"You oughta come out here," Drew hollers. "There's a ton of them, and they're bigger'n that minnow you just pulled in."

"I'm fine where I am!" I yell, and turn back to the fish. The fish that could not possibly have said what I thought it said.

Maybe it was some weird wheezy kind of fish-stress I heard. Can fish wheeze through their gills?

But it was so clear. *Release me . . . and I will grant you a wish.*

Maybe it's not a real fish. Maybe it's like that singing fish on the wall decoration—what song did it sing? Whatever.

Maybe this is like . . . a fake fish meant to advertise the tournament. It's for the Make-a-Wish foundation after all. I want so much to convince myself of this, but when I look down, the fish in my hand is still slimy and flopping, and there is nothing battery-operated about it.

But it's quiet now.

I must have imagined the voice. I have magic flowers and crystal dresses and wishes swirling around my brain, and that all added up to a fish talking. Which it couldn't have.

Even though Drew says Billy'll take the fish, it's definitely too small to keep—wish or no wish. I lean over the hole to drop it in. The sun catches its bright-green eye, and I hesitate.

I *could* make a wish just for fun, the way you wish on your birthday candles or shooting stars. In September, when I blew out the twelve candles on my cake, I wished for Roberto Sullivan to fall in love with me. It was silly, and of course, it didn't happen. Roberto has curly black hair, dark-brown eyes, and dimples. He's the cutest boy in our whole school. I blew out every single candle, and Roberto still doesn't even know my name. But there's no harm in wishing.

"Let Roberto Sullivan fall in love with me," I whisper to the fish. Drew cheers, and I look up to see him reeling in another fish that's five times the size of this tiny thing in my mitten. I have to laugh. "And while you're at it, make me not afraid of the ice. No offense, but I want to go out where the real fish are."

I drop the fish back into the hole. It flicks its tail and disappears into the dark, and I feel a shiver that has nothing to do with the bite in the air. It rushes through me—prickly and electric—and rattles me from my ear-flapped hat to my almost-numb toes.

I look out at the ice where Drew and Mrs. McNeill are sitting, over the deeper water. It actually looks okay out there. Like a perfectly safe place to catch fish.

I gather up my bucket and my rod and start out toward them.

"Hey, chicken! You finally coming out to where the fish are?" Drew calls.

And I stop. Because it's weird. I *don't* feel like a chicken anymore. I'm not afraid.

I look down through the clear, dark ice. The water is deeper here, probably over my head. But it doesn't bother me at all.

I take a step and wait for the fear. It doesn't come.

It's impossible, but it's so.

I take another step. And another. I keep going, ready to feel the wobble in my knees, the flip in my stomach, the thin-ice, catch-in-my-breath fear. It doesn't come. When I stop beside Drew, I'm almost afraid of how not-afraid I am.

What happened? What did that fish *do*?

"Dude, you can't fish right on top of me." Drew looks up, frowning, and points out past his nana. "Have her drill you a hole out there."

I walk farther out. The ice crackles and thumps. And now I can hear it the way Mrs. McNeill does, like music. Otherworldly and peaceful and wild.

"Coming out where the action is?" Mrs. McNeill sets her rod in a holder and helps me drill a fresh fishing hole about ten feet from hers. Almost the second I drop my line, I feel a tug, and I pull in a perch.

"Woo-hoo! Now she's got it!" Mrs. McNeill cheers.

I lift the fish to take the hook out. It's bigger than the first little one I caught. The one that . . . I still can't quite figure what happened. Did it talk? It couldn't have. And the wish thing . . . I look around, half expecting to see Roberto Sullivan heading out onto the ice with a dozen roses, but he's not here. It must be that I'm just getting used to the ice.

This new fish is quiet. It has the same slimy stripes but regular beady fish eyes. I drop it in the keep bucket and rebait my hook.

By the time the sun is overhead, I've got half a bucket full of good, quiet fish who don't make promises—other than to help me raise money for my dress. I almost forget about the wish fish until we're walking back to shore.

"You certainly came around," Mrs. McNeill says. "When we first went out, you were so nervous I thought you'd be hugging the shore all day."

"Yeah." I remember that feeling, walking over the ice now. But it's gone. Like magic.

Mrs. McNeill invites me to stay for lunch, so I call Mom to let her know. When we finish our hot chicken soup, we bundle up and walk to Billy's place. He's excited because now he can offer fish fry tonight, and usually it's only on weekends. He puts a crisp five dollar bill in my hand, along with two dollars and a couple of quarters. I shove the money into my snow pants pocket and zip it shut. It's only seven fifty, but it's a start.

"You have good morning fishing?" Mr. Beleko is drying glasses with a towel at the bar. He's my friend Dasha's father. Their family moved here last year from Ukraine. Dasha's mom does something with computers and works at a software company across town, but this was the only job Mr. Beleko could find. Back in Ukraine, he was a lawyer, but I guess certifications and stuff are different here, so he works with Billy for now. He's learning English along with Dasha and her little brother, Alex.

"It was a great morning," I say. And I mean it. "Is Dasha going to be at dance today?"

He nods. "She been practicing all week. Always stepping and kicking and stomping." He shakes his head, but I know he loves that Dasha is taking Irish dance lessons. He always taps his foot to the music when he's waiting to pick her up.

"See you later!" I wave to Billy and Mr. Beleko and do a few jig steps on my way out the door. The fish fry quarters jingle in my pocket all the way home.

When I say good-bye to Drew and his nana and open our kitchen door, it's after three. Abby's at the table eating cereal with a spoon but no milk. She's had stomach problems since she was little, so the list of things-Abby-can't-eat is like ten miles long. "Hey, chick!" She shakes the box at me. "Want some breakfast?"

"Most of the world is done with lunch, Ab. But thanks. Guess what?" I pull the fish money from my pocket and tell her about my plan to earn money for a better solo dress.

"How come they're so expensive?" she asks, tipping her bowl up to get the last of the frosted crumbs.

"Because they have to be really sparkly, with crystals and stuff."

"Can't you sparkle-dazzle it with sequins from the craft store and call it a day? I'd totally help."

That makes me laugh because Abby is not the crafting type. She tried to make her own evil queen Halloween costume a few years ago and ended up looking like she lost a fight with a glue gun. If her costume disaster had happened to me, I would have stayed home, but Abby wore it to the school dance anyway and didn't care what anybody thought.

"We could do it ourselves. It'd be fun!" Abby makes a gun shape with her hands and pretends she's shooting sequins at me. "Pshew! Pshew! You know I'm the fastest sparkle-dazzler east of the Mississippi, right?"

I make a sparkle-dazzle gun with my hands too, and point at her. "There ain't room for two of us in this town, pardner." I heard something like that on one of Drew's Westerns once.

Abby puts her hands up and laughs. "I surrender to your sparkly talents." For a minute, I feel like I have my sister back.

I help her clear her lunch/breakfast stuff from the table. "We missed you last night. Where'd you go?"

"Just a party." She shrugs. "Why? Did Mom and Dad say something?"

"No. I just wondered. Were you with Kira and Jess?"

"Nah. I don't really hang out with people from high school anymore. This was a Tony's thing." Tony's is the pizza place where Abby waitresses. She looks at her watch. "Speaking of that, I better get ready. I have the dinner shift. And Mom asked if I'd drop you off at dance."

"I'll get my stuff." I go to my room, put on leggings and a T-shirt, and grab my dance bag.

When I come downstairs, Abby grabs her purse and keys, and we head out to Scarlett, which is what Abby calls the rusty red Honda she inherited from Dad.

There's a tiny waxed-paper bag on the passenger seat, like the kind they use at Regal Bakery when they give you extra cinnamon sugar to sprinkle on your donuts. It still has a few light-brown powdery crumbs in it. "Hey!" I pick up the bag and hold it as if it's evidence. "Did you get cinnamon donuts without me?"

Abby snatches the bag from me and shoves it into her jacket pocket. "No, that's Seth's."

"Who's Seth?"

"One of the cooks." She backs out of the driveway and heads toward downtown. She glances over at me. "You should see how high he can throw the pizza dough and still catch it. And hey . . . we *should* get donuts! We can go later if you want. They have a bakery on campus, but it's not the same."

"Nothing's as good as Regal. But don't you work until nine? They'll be closed."

"Yeah . . . well, tomorrow then."

When we get to Brigid's School of Irish Dance, Abby drops me off. "Dad's picking you up after, right?"

"Yep." I grab my bag from the backseat, wrap my scarf around my face, and run across the windy parking lot to catch up with Dasha, who's just heading inside. "Hey! How's your vacation going?"

"Good!"

She opens the door and a rush of warm air greets us. It always smells great at the dance studio—a mix of wood floors and Miss Brigid's tangy perfume, plus old books and pencils, since this building used to be a school.

"What have you been doing all week?" I ask as we head for the benches.

"I make new app. Want to see?" She pulls her phone from her coat pocket, taps a few things, and hands it to me.

There's a super-simple video game on the screen. It's like Pong, the old Atari game Dad likes to talk about, from when he was a kid and video games were a new thing. "Cool! How do I get the paddles to move?"

"Tip it. Game uses phone's . . . how is it called . . . accelerometer?" Dasha's in the coding club at our school. She may still be struggling with some parts of English, but she understands computer stuff better than anybody. I guess coding and math are international languages.

That's actually how Dasha and I got to be friends. On one of her first days at our school last year, my friend Catherine had a trombone lesson during math class, so I didn't have a partner and ended up working with Dasha. She was just starting to learn English, but she was so good at the equations we were doing. Algebra isn't really my thing, but somehow, even without speaking much English, Dasha helped me understand it better. I invited her to sit with Catherine and me at lunch, and then we started Irish dance class together and have been friends ever since. She's been trying to get me to join the coding club, but that's definitely a language I don't speak yet.

The game she made is cool, though. I play until I tip the phone too much, and Dasha's electronic dot flies past my paddle. "I need more practice." I give her the phone, and we sit down to put on our hard shoes. They're kind of like tap shoes, with hard fiberglass heels and tips to make noise on the floor. "I hope we can move up to Novice soon." I tighten my laces and fasten the strap that goes over my ankle. "You're doing the Montreal feis, right?"

Dasha nods. "If my mother does not work."

"My mom can take us both as long as your mom writes a note so we can cross the border. You have to go so we can move up to Novice together. Then we'll be in class with Catherine."

Catherine and I have been friends since kindergarten, but we only have one class together at school this year. It'd be great if she and Dasha and I could all dance together. Even if Catherine moves up again soon, at least we'll still be with some other people our age. Most of the kids in Advanced Beginner are younger than Dasha and me, since we've only been dancing a year.

"Come on in, and let's warm up with some trebles," Miss Brigid calls from the studio door.

Dasha and I file in with the rest of our class. The littler kids are all stomping around as if they're Godzilla. Irish dance shoes make you feel big that way.

"Let's have quiet feet now so we can start!" Miss Brigid calls out. "One, two, ready, go . . . Tre-ble one! Tre-ble two . . ." We kick-click-shuffle-back our feet, inching toward the big mirror up front. "Keep those shoulders back."

When we finish, Miss Brigid heads for the music player. "Okay, treble jig now!" The song starts—all lively accordion notes until our feet start moving to provide the percussion. We sound like a giant's typewriter—clicks and clacks and stomps bouncing off the cinderblock walls, so loud I feel our footsteps vibrating in my chest.

"Can you see your feet in the mirror?" Miss Brigid shouts over the music. "Turn your heel out and open up those hips. Good, Charlie!"

We run through the dance three more times, getting more confident with our steps until the sound of our shoes stomping in unison shakes the room like thunder. This is what I love most about Irish dance—holding my arms at my sides, kicking and shuffling and hopping until I'm all stomped out.

When class ends, we scatter to the orange chairs that line the walls and take off our shoes. Catherine and the other Novice kids are coming in now. Dasha and I wave to Catherine. She starts to wave back, but then a toddler runs by—somebody's little sister—and Catherine gets this panicked look on her face and races out of the room.

"I hope she is all right," Dasha says.

"She's fine." I laugh because I know exactly what happened. "She forgot her flour baby in the car again." Catherine has home and career skills class this quarter, which means she has to carry a five-pound bag of flour around for ten weeks, pretending it's a baby. She was really excited for the project. She named her bag of flour Meredith and dressed it in a purple onesie and a bunny rabbit bib, but she's so busy with dance and band and stuff that she keeps leaving her baby places. Last week, she abandoned it in the bathroom overnight, so her little sister kidnapped it and left a ransom note. Catherine had to pay five dollars to get Meredith back.

In a minute, Catherine comes back out of breath, hugging her flour baby to her chest. "Sorry—I forgot she was in the backseat," she says. "I'm lucky Mom got talking in the parking lot and hadn't left yet." Catherine hurries to put on her dance shoes, while Dasha and I change back to our sneakers.

I'm tying my laces when Miss Brigid taps me on the shoulder. "Are your parents here? I wanted to talk with them about the possibility of switching classes if things go well at the Montreal feis. You too, Dasha. I expect to see you both with medals later this month."

"I hope so!" Dasha and I need a first, second, or third place for every dance at the Advanced Beginner level to move up to Novice.

"I'd also like you to think about the Albany feis coming up in April," Miss Brigid says, and floats off to talk with one of the Novice parents.

"Woo-hoo!" I raise a hand, and Dasha high-fives me. "When we move into the next class, we'll get to learn clicks—those are so cool—and we'll be in class with Catherine, and you know what? The three of us should dance in the talent show in May!"

Dasha looks down at her shoes. "Talent show people must also introduce at microphone, no? I do not think I will be ready for that."

"Of course you will! You're doing great."

Dasha smiles, shrugs, and gets up to go. I can't imagine being plunked into a new place where I couldn't understand half of what people were saying. She's super smart, and she's learned a ton. But I guess it's hard.

I'm thinking about how I could help Dasha—we could practice the kind of introduction you have to do at the talent show—when one of the Novice dancers runs through with her new solo dress to show Miss Brigid. It's white with different-colored crystals all down the front. A green flash catches my eye, and I remember that little fish from the ice.

It was like something out of a fairy tale. It couldn't have been real.

But somehow, I really did lose my fear of the ice. How did that happen so fast? I spent the whole afternoon out there and didn't worry once about being swallowed up. Maybe it really was a wish fish.

Then I remember I made a two-part wish. And Roberto Sullivan hasn't called or anything.

I watch Miss Brigid gushing over the girl's shiny new dress. The crystals sparkle as if they're magic.

And I can't decide if I believe, or not.

Chapter 4

The Second Wish

Abby's riding back to college with her friend Kallie, so early Monday morning, she and Dad pile her winter clothes and Christmas gifts into Kallie's mom's minivan. Denver whines the whole time; he hates it when anybody goes anywhere.

"Sorry, buddy. I'll see you for spring break." Abby rubs noses with Denver and then says good-bye to the rest of us.

"Don't forget to text me this semester," I tell her. "Even if you're busy. At least send me some cool pictures of college things."

Abby laughs. "Like what? Stacks of books and bad dining hall food?"

"Anything is more exciting than middle school cafeteria goulash." I give her a tight hug and breathe in the smell of her apple shampoo. I wish she didn't have to go back.

But break is over. So Abby and Kallie head back across the lake to the University of Vermont for second semester, and I ride to school with Mom and Dad.

The first day back from vacation is always rough. Everybody's spent the break eating pie and watching TV and forgetting how to solve equations. Roberto Sullivan walks past me in the hall with his flour baby tucked under his arm like a football. He's half-asleep and definitely not in love with me. Only Mrs. Racette seems to have held on to her pre-vacation enthusiasm.

"Today's the day you've all been waiting for," she announces as we settle in for eighth-period life science. This is my only class with Catherine, but she's absent, and there's a weird kid with shaggy red hair sitting next to me in her seat. I think he might have been in my art class last year, but he was quiet. And he's grown since then. He's so tall and skinny he looks like a clay project somebody stretched out too much. He keeps staring at me. I frown at him, and he looks away.

"I'm passing out registration forms for the regional science fair," Mrs. Racette says.

"*Pssst!*" the weird kid whispers.

He's holding out a folded paper. I take it from him, thinking it's a sign-in sheet for attendance or something, but when I open it, it's full of hearts and dragon drawings. One of the dragons has a fiery speech bubble that says, "Will you go out with me?"

What?!

I'm afraid to look up because I can feel the kid still star-ing at me, and on top of that, Mrs. Racette probably saw him pass the note, which I took because I couldn't have guessed in a million years it was going to be a dragon ask-ing me out. What if she takes it and reads it to the class? And who *is* that kid? I don't even know him.

"The fair is May second, beginning at nine in the morning," Mrs. Racette says. Thankfully, she missed the note-pass.

"Psst! I read about your project from last year in the school paper," the weird kid whispers across the aisle. He smiles the goofiest smile ever, showing off every one of his braces-covered teeth. "I thought it was wonderful."

Sure he did. He wasn't the one known as Pooper Scoo-per the rest of the year.

"Thanks," I whisper. But my face is burning. Where did this kid come from? And what am I supposed to do about this dragon?

"You can choose a research project or technology dem-onstration," Mrs. Racette goes on. "I'll give you time to think, and we'll talk more next week."

I turn away from the dragon boy and pretend to be super-interested in what Liza and Paige are saying about plant-growth experiments. When class is almost over, I whisper to Paige, "Hey . . . do you have any idea who that is in Catherine's seat today?"

She looks up at the dragon kid. "That's Bobby O'Sullivan. He's in coding club with my brother."

"Do you like to work with computers too?" Bobby has appeared at my side.

"No," I say. He looks as if this is the worst news he's heard all year.

"I bet you'd love it," he says. "You should come to a club meeting sometime!"

"I . . . uh . . . I'm pretty busy."

"Here." Bobby grabs the dragon note from my desk and scribbles something under the flames. "You can call me if you have any questions about when we meet or anything."

"Uh. Okay. Thanks." This is so weird. I look down at the paper, and see that he's written his name and phone number. But he hasn't written Bobby. He's written Robert.

I look up. "Your name is Robert?"

He nods. "You can call me Robert or Bobby. Either one. You can call me whatever you want, really." He smiles.

Bobby O'Sullivan the dragon boy is *Robert* O'Sullivan.

Robert O'Sullivan, who does not have curly hair or dimples, and who is most definitely *not* Roberto Sullivan. But who seems to like me a whole lot, all of a sudden.

"Want me to carry your books?" he asks hopefully.

"No thank you." I practically run out the door, and I can't concentrate the rest of the day. The whole time we're talking about causes of the American Revolution in history and equations in math and self-portrait styles in art, I am thinking about that fish.

I come to two conclusions:

#1: It wasn't just me getting used to the ice. That wish fish was the real thing.

#2: It is important to speak *very* clearly when you're asking a fish for something.

After school, I walk down to the nurse's office so Mom can give me a ride home.

She's typing at her computer. "Give me ten minutes to finish this application, okay?"

I swipe a granola bar from the stash in her Band-Aid cupboard. "Application for what?"

"A full-time position opened at the high school. Mrs. Larkner decided not to come back after she had her baby."

"So you wouldn't work here anymore? Who's going to be my granola bar supplier?"

Mom laughs. "You'll be okay." Her fingers fly over the keyboard. "This would really help with the college fund."

"I know. I was just kidding." College is super expensive. I heard Mom and Dad talking when Abby's tuition bill came.

"And . . . submit." Mom takes a deep breath. "Keep your fingers crossed."

"I will," I promise. But on the way across the snowy parking lot, I think about a different kind of luck. What if I catch the fish again and wish—very clearly and carefully—for Mom to get the full-time job? Then we'd have more money for college *and* dance dresses.

By the time I finish my homework, Drew and his nana are waiting by the rocks. It snowed a little last night, so there's a sugar-sprinkle of white powder over the frozen lake.

"I was out earlier, and they're biting deep today," Mrs. McNeill says. "We may need to head out a bit farther."

I nod and follow her and Drew, walking the sled's track as if it's a balance beam. The ice is talking again . . . burping out gurgles and whooshes as air bubbles escape. I wait for my heart to beat faster. I wait for my throat to tighten with fear. I wait for my stomach to twist and my knees to wobble. But none of that happens. I just walk, one foot in front of the other, until we're almost halfway to the island a mile offshore.

Mrs. McNeill drills the first hole, looks down, and nods. "Gained another inch or two last night. Gonna be a good long season."

Drew and I use the power auger to drill ourselves holes. Then we drop our lines and wait.

"What would you do if killer bees came after us right now?" Drew asks, bouncing his pole a little.

"I wouldn't have to do anything. It's five below zero out here," I say. "The bees would freeze."

"What if it were summer?"

"I'd jump in the lake and hide underwater."

"Wrong!" Drew shouts.

"Shhh!" Mrs. McNeill whispers. "You'll scare the fish."

"Sorry," Drew says, and turns to me. "Killer bees know when you're hiding underwater and will wait for you to surface to breathe. You gotta run instead."

"You can outrun killer bees?"

Drew nods. "Well, most people can. Probably not me. I'd be stung to death."

Drew's not exactly athletic. He's one of the tallest kids in our grade, though, so everybody's always asking him why he doesn't play basketball. His dad is actually *making* him try out for the school team this winter. Drew hates the practices and can't wait for the coach to make cuts at the end of the month.

"Maybe that'll be the silver lining of basketball practice," I say. "Developing speed to outrun the bees."

Drew shakes his head. "It's hopeless. I can't even—hey! Got a bite!" He tugs on the line, but the fish gets away. Right away, he catches another one, though, and pretty soon, we're all reeling in perch. But in a few minutes, it's quiet again.

"Well, that didn't last," Mrs. McNeill says. "Let's give it a bit and see if they start again."

I sit on my bucket with my bait in the water. Even with the ice making its thundery sounds, it's peaceful here. Somehow, ultra-cold weather makes the sky bluer and the clouds whiter. Being out on the lake today, in the wind-whoosh quiet, feels like visiting a faraway crystal world, even though I can see our neighborhood when I look toward shore.

The ice feels so different now, and this feeling—the *not* being scared—makes me think even more about that little fish with the green eyes. I guess it wasn't a dream or my imagination.

It's so weird. But if it wasn't real, that Bobby-Robert-O'Sullivan kid wouldn't have written me the note. If it wasn't real, I couldn't feel this way now, not after being scared of the ice my whole life. And if the fairy-tale fish *was* real, then somewhere under the snow-dusted ice it's still swimming around, waiting to be caught, waiting to grant another wish.

"I'm going to try moving in toward shore," I say, and start to move my gear.

"Ain't gonna help," Drew says, in his best cowboy drawl.

"*Isn't*," Mrs. McNeill says. "But he's probably right." She looks up at the clouds. "Low pressure system coming in. They're probably done biting for tonight."

"That's okay," I say. "I'd still like to try."

Mrs. McNeill nods. "Just watch that ridge," she says, pointing to a place where the ice has buckled up a bit. It looks like a plate tectonics picture we saw in science last year. "The ice around it may not be as strong."

I keep my distance from the ridge, even though it doesn't look like there's anything wrong with the ice around it. When I get to my hole from yesterday, it's iced over a little. I poke through the surface with the end of my pole to open things up. As soon as I drop the line in the water, there's a little tug.

I give the pole a quick pull and start reeling. Whatever is on the hook feels like it can't weigh more than a butterfly, and for a second, I think I imagined that tug. But then I pull it up from the ice hole—the fish with the emerald eyes.

I can hear Drew and his nana laughing, so I look up to see if they've noticed. But they're focused on something in the bait bucket. I turn back to the fish on my line. Slowly, I reach down, wrap my mitten around its flapping body, and take it off the hook.

The fish doesn't say anything. It flicks its tail hard and slips out of my hands onto the ice. It flops around, leaving a frantic trail of fish prints in the new snow. I kneel down and cup my hands around it until I can pick it back up. And when I stand, I hear it.

"Please . . . release me. And I will grant you a wish."

It is the same raspy voice, all throaty and chilled. This time I know it's not coming from Drew or his nana or my imagination. It's real. And knowing that makes me hesitate in wishing.

This fall in English class, we had a short story unit about wishes. In all those stories—"The Rocking-Horse Winner" and "The Monkey's Paw" and that old Russian folktale about the fisherman and his wife—the people were greedy or stupid or both, and their wishes went horribly wrong. Wishing could seriously wreck your life if you weren't careful.

The fish flops in my hand, and my heart speeds up. I'm not afraid of the ice anymore; I'm afraid of the wishing. Before, when I wished for confidence on the frozen lake, I never thought I'd get it. Since I did, the wishing is different. This time, I know I may get what I'm asking for—or something that sounds like it, anyway. I can't help worrying I'll ask for the wrong thing.

Is Mom's full-time nursing job a greedy wish? I'm wishing for someone else, but the truth is, I know that extra money will make my life better. Does that make it selfish?

I look at the fish in my hand. It's not flopping anymore, just staring up at me with its sparkly green eyes. I need to hurry up and wish or it's going to suffocate and die, and who knows what'll happen then? The people in the stories never killed their magical fish.

I take a deep breath. The fish was okay with me wishing

not to be afraid on the ice, after all, and that was a little self-ish. It didn't exactly deliver Roberto with love notes, and Bobby O'Sullivan is kind of annoying, but the wish wasn't a total disaster. It's probably just wishing for piles of gold that makes the magic feel like it *really* needs to teach you a lesson.

"Please let my mom get a full-time job," I whisper. I'm about to let the fish go when I realize there are all sorts of ways for that wish to go wrong. I could go home and find out she's been hired as a full-time garbage collector or lion tamer at the circus. "And when I say 'full-time job,' I mean the exact nursing job she applied for on her computer this afternoon," I add, and drop the fish into the hole.

For a second, it just floats there, and I'm afraid I killed it by waffling so long about my wish. But then it twitches, and with a flick of its tail, turns and darts into the darkness.

"Any luck over there?" Mrs. McNeill calls. She and Drew are pulling the sled, heading in toward shore.

"Just a little one," I say, loading my bucket and rod onto the sled. "Not worth keeping."

The sky's getting dark and it's starting to snow as we walk back. Lights are on in the houses. I can see Drew's parents in the kitchen, and I wonder what Mom's doing at our house right now. I wonder if the phone is ringing. And if my wish for her job will come true.

Chapter 5

A Fish and a Feis

When I get home, Dad's dumping pasta into a pot of boiling water, and Mom's making a salad. She doesn't look especially excited, but I ask anyway. "Any news on the job?"

"That application deadline was only an hour ago, Charlie." She laughs and slices a cucumber into the bowl. A piece bounces off the edge, onto the floor, and Denver scarfs it up—the canine vacuum cleaner. "The committee would have to be magic to have gone through all those applications and made a decision already."

I panic for a second when she says the word "magic." Could she know about my fish somehow? But Mom doesn't look up from the salad. "I'll find out when I find out," she says.

I look at her phone and feel impatient it's not ringing. My ice fear vanished the second I let the fish go. And even though he's the wrong boy, Bobby O'Sullivan showed up pretty fast too. If nothing's happening with Mom's job yet, does that mean the fish-wish didn't work this time? Or do some wishes take longer than others?

"I'm thinking of a word," Mom says.

"Peppermint?" I guess.

"Nope. Diminutive," Dad says.

"You're both wrong. It was place setting." She nods toward the cupboard. "Set the table, will you, Charlie?"

"I win," I say, pulling silverware from the drawer. "You need a place setting to serve Peppermint Patties."

"Not likely," Dad says, throwing a piece of spaghetti against the cupboard to see if it's done. It sticks. "But you could have a diminutive place setting for a mouse or other small rodent."

"A mouse eating a Peppermint Pattie."

"I declare a tie." Mom hands Dad the colander and peels the spaghetti off the cupboard.

"That's lame. And technically, place setting is two words anyway." I check the refrigerator calendar on my way to the table. "Who's taking me to Montreal for the feis at the end of the month?" I ask.

"I am," Mom says, handing me the salad dressing. "That's the weekend Dad's skiing with his old college roommate."

Mom's phone rings then, and I try not to look too excited when she answers it. It's not the job, though—just Abby.

"But I put money in your account last week," Mom says, motioning for us to start eating. She listens, then sighs. "No, if the professor says you need the book, get it. We'll take care of it. Okay . . . Love you. Bye." She comes to the table shaking her head. "One chemistry textbook, two hundred dollars. Let's hope that new job comes through."

It's a week and a half before Mom's phone rings with good news. She hangs up and dances around the kitchen with the pizza we brought home. "I got the job!"

"Congratulations! When do you start?" Dad leans in to kiss her on the cheek.

"Monday." She turns to me. "Isn't that great, Charlie?"

"Yeah! Congrats, Mom." I high-five her, but now I can't stop thinking about the fish. I was starting to wonder if it was out of magic when Mom's phone call didn't come right away.

I haven't caught the fish again since I wished for Mom's nursing job, but I haven't really tried either.

Every time I walk by that shallow spot by the point, I think about it. But for now, I don't need any more wishes. I've been out with Drew and Mrs. McNeill almost every day. We've been going out deeper and having plenty of luck with regular fish. Mrs. McNeill said one of my perch might have a chance at the tournament prize, but when we took it in to be weighed, it was half a pound smaller than the current front-runner. We've been taking our fish to Billy's every day, though, so my dress fund is up to forty-seven dollars on top of the three hundred Mom and Dad said they'd pay.

"Hey, Mom, do you think we could go up to Montreal early on the day of the feis? That way I'll have plenty of time to choose my new solo dress before I dance."

"I don't see why not," she says, opening the pizza box and taking a piece of pepperoni.

"Can we give Dasha a ride? She's not sure her mom will be able to get time off work."

"Sure."

"Perfect!" I slide a piece of pizza onto my plate and do some math in my head.

The feis is a little over two weeks away. If I don't have too much homework and the weather's okay, that's fourteen more fishing days. One of those days, I might pull in a perch big enough to win the Make-a-Wish tournament. And even if I don't, if I can catch three or four pounds a day, that'll add up at Billy's.

Maybe if I find a nice used dress at a good price, I'll get one of the hair pieces to go with it. The advanced Irish dance girls wear fancy wigs, all piled up with bouncy curls that match the color of their hair. The long, full wigs cost hundreds of dollars, but they also make littler ones—ponytails and buns that you clip onto your hair. Maybe I could afford one of those.

"Charlie, you still with us?" Dad waves a hand in front of my face. "You look like you're a million miles away."

"Sorry, I was just thinking. I'm happy for Mom with the new job." I polish off my slice of pizza and reach for a second. "Also, I'm thinking of a word."

"Persnickety?" Dad says, making a face that matches his guess.

"Great word," I say, "but no."

"Let's see," Mom says. "My guess is rutabaga."

"Nope! It was sparkle," I say. "Dad wins. Because persnickety is a more sparkly word than rutabaga." Besides, I don't really know what a rutabaga looks like, and I'm too excited to think about vegetables when there are dresses and dances and medals to dream about.

Mom sighs. "Rutabagas never get the respect they deserve."

On Friday, I stay after with Mrs. Racette to look up science project ideas, but I can't find anything interesting that doesn't also have bad-nickname potential. Then Bobby O'Sullivan shows up, all out of breath.

"I left coding club early so I could talk to you. Want to be science fair partners?" he asks.

"Um . . . I can't. Sorry. I'm already working with some-one," I say, even though I'm not exactly. I was *thinking* about talking to Dasha and Catherine. That must count.

Bobby looks crushed, but only for a second. "Well, if you need anything, any help or anything, just let me know. I'm good at posters and stuff. And I can program too." He pulls out his phone and taps it to launch an app he must have made in coding club. It's a digital fireworks display, and at the end the sparkles all dance around and settle into letters that spell . . . oh no . . .

i love charlie

"I have to go, Mrs. Racette. I'll do more research at home." I hurry down the hall and wonder how long it takes a wish to wear off.

Dasha had coding club after school too, but she's not in our hallway yet, so I wait at her locker. I'm excited to tell her about Mom's new job and let her know we're going up early to go dress shopping before the feis. I really need to get some advice on Bobby O'Sullivan too. But when Dasha shows up, her cheeks are shiny with tears. "What's wrong? Did something happen at coding club?"

She blinks fast a few times and shakes her head. "No. I went to check on my score for language test today. I study so hard, but . . ." She shakes her head again, and I know that she's failed another one of those exams they give students studying English as a Second Language to see if they're ready to move into regular classes.

"Aw, Dasha, it'll be okay. You'll get it." I put an arm around her. "You're really smart. You're a brainiac at coding, and you always get a hundred in math."

She sighs. "But other classes . . ." She shakes her head. "Words go by too fast." Dasha wipes her tears away and sniffs. "Sorry. We talk about something else now?"

"Okay." I tell her about Mom's job and Bobby O'Sullivan's fireworks. I don't tell her about the fish that made those things happen, though. Some secrets are too weird even for best friends.

We talk about the feis as we head down the hall. Dasha nods and smiles and looks excited, but I can tell she's still upset about that test.

Dasha laughed about Bobby O'Sullivan but didn't really have any advice, so when I get home, I text Abby. She's always had boys asking her out, so she must know how to handle these things.

Charlie: Hey, are you there?
Abby: On my way to class. Wassup?
Charlie: I have this thing going on with a boy who
          likes me.

Abby: Cool!!!!!

Charlie: No! Not cool!

Abby: ????

Charlie: I don't like him, but he keeps sending me notes
　　　　　and making me apps and stuff.

Abby: OMG he's making you apps?! LOL

Charlie: It's not funny, it's weird. What should I do?

Abby: If you don't like him, tell him you just want to be
　　　　friends.

Charlie: I thought I did that, but . . .

Abby: Gotta run. Calc's starting.

Charlie: Will you be around later?

I watch the screen for a minute, but she doesn't answer, so I change into warm clothes, put on my winter stuff, and run to Drew's house. He and his nana are outside loading the sled.

"Hello there, Miss Charlie!" Mrs. McNeill calls. "Fishing for crystals again?"

"Yep. I have two more weeks before my feis." Mrs. McNeill thinks it's crazy how much the solo dresses cost, but she's been helping me out. Every once in a while, she sneaks one of her fish into my bucket when Drew's not looking.

"Nooo . . . not another feece!" Drew clutches his face with his hands, drops to the ground, and rolls in the snow, pretending to be in agony. "The feces . . . they are boring me to death!"

"Is Rachael going?" I ask, and then realize it's a dumb question. She's at the Prizewinner level—that's above Novice—and she goes to pretty much every feis on the East Coast.

Drew ignores my question anyway and keeps rolling around moaning.

"You'll have to forgive him," Mrs. McNeill whispers. "Rough afternoon at basketball practice. Final tryouts and cuts are coming up, and his father's putting on the heat."

"Dad's so excited about the tryouts he got me new basketball shoes that cost like a hundred fifty dollars." Drew sighs. I feel bad for him. Those shoes aren't going to solve anything. "And if I get cut, I'm still not off the hook." He looks over at the fishing poles. "Ha! Off the hook, get it?" He kicks at the snow. "Dad says if I don't make this team, I gotta try out for baseball or something."

"Does it have to be a sport?" I ask. "Science fair is sort of extracurricular, and we get extra credit if we do it."

"Nah. If I did science fair, Dad would find a way to make that about sports too. I'd end up studying how many granola bars a guy can eat before he pukes during a workout or something." He starts pulling the sled toward the frozen lake. "Let's fish."

It's been on the warm side this week, and today is the first day it's dropped back into single digits, so the ice is talking again. We're walking by the point when I see the hole from our first week of fishing, all frozen over. I stop. "Mrs. McNeill? Can you help me open up this hole again?"

"You chickening out?" Drew makes *bawk-bawk*ing noises for a few seconds until his nana gives him the stop-it look.

"No." I'm fine with going out farther now, but I've been thinking all afternoon about Dasha and the test that made her so sad. "I want to fish here for a while. Then I'll come out."

Mrs. McNeill fires up the auger, drills through the frozen circle of ice, and leaves me a bucket and a rod with a lure on it because the bait shop was out of minnows. The lure looks more like a silver feather than a fish, so I'm not expecting much when I lower it into the hole.

But apparently, any magic fish dumb enough to get caught in the same spot three times is also dumb enough to think a piece of shiny metal might be good to eat. The tug comes right away, and I reel in the fish.

Same sparkling eye.

Same raspy voice.

"Release me . . . and I will grant you a wish."

Chapter 6

The Third and Fourth Wishes

"Please let . . ."

I'm about to wish for Dasha's English to get better, for her to pass that awful test so she can be in classes with me. But then I realize this is the third time I've caught the wish fish. This fish didn't say anything about a limit, but in stories about genies, the third wish is pretty much the end of the road. (My first two-part wish, about Roberto and my fear of the ice, only counts as one, I think. Especially since the real Roberto Sullivan still doesn't know I exist.)

What I really want is to make this one a triple wish. *Please let Dasha learn English faster so she can pass her test, and please let Drew be awesome at his basketball tryouts so he'll make the team and then his dad will leave him alone, and please let Dasha and me both place in the top three in our feis so we can move up to Novice.* But maybe it was the double wishing that first time that made the fish mess up with Roberto. So I decide to stick with a single wish.

"Please let Dasha pass her language test," I whisper, and I let the fish go. I'm tempted to stick the lure right back into the water to see if I can catch it again and make Drew's basketball wish, but that seems like it might push a magic fish over the edge.

I pack up and walk out to where Drew and Mrs. McNeill are sitting. "How's it going?"

Drew grunts.

"Slow," Mrs. McNeill says, bobbing her pole up and down. "But feel free to join us." She nods toward the auger, and I use it to drill myself a hole. The auger blade spins, and it sinks in, leaving a shiny donut of shaved ice around the hole. It takes a while to hit water; the ice must be at least twelve inches thick by now.

I sit down on my bucket, drop a line, and pull out my phone to try Abby again.

Charlie: Is your class over? I need advice.

Abby doesn't text back right away, so I put my phone back in my pocket. Pretty soon, we all start getting bites.

"You must be our good-luck charm, Miss Charlie!" Mrs. McNeill says, using a pair of pliers to twist her lure out of a fish's mouth.

"What about your four-leaf clover charm?" I ask, laughing.

She shakes her head, dropping her line back in. "I'm wearing it, but it wasn't doing a thing for me until you showed up."

The fish only bite for about half an hour. By the time it slows down, it's getting dark anyway, so we head in to shore and deliver our fish to Billy.

Mrs. McNeill says it again. "Charlie's our lucky charm!"

"Thanks." I smile and accept my twelve dollars for today's perch, feeling just as lucky as she says I am. In fact, I feel downright sparkly.

My sparkly luck hangs in there for most of January. The weather's been great for fishing, with cold nights so the ice gets thicker and sunny days so the fish can see the lures. By the week of the feis, I have more than four hundred fifty dollars for my solo dress.

"Do you think I should go with blue or orange?" I ask Dasha as we're lacing up our soft shoes at dance on Sunday. "Mom says blue matches my eyes, but I like how bright the orange dresses are."

"I think both look nice," Dasha says.

"Let's go, ladies and gentlemen!" Miss Brigid shouts. "Line up and we'll start with a reel."

I find a spot in front of the mirror between Dasha and Chloe. We reel and slip jig through the first half hour of class and then switch shoes for the treble jig and hornpipe.

"Point your toe on the hop!" Miss Brigid calls over the music. "Straighten that knee!"

When class ends, Dasha and I change into our sneakers while the Novice kids get ready. We're staying to watch their class so we can see what it'll be like when we move up.

"Are you guys in Novice now?" Catherine pulls her wheeled dance bag up beside us, sits down on it, and starts putting on her hard shoes.

"Not yet," I say. "But hopefully after the Montreal feis."

"You'll make it," Catherine says. She finishes lacing her shoe, straps the buckle over her ankle, and hurries across the room to stand by Isabelle for the start of class. Then she races back to her dance bag.

"Catherine, we're ready to begin. Is there a problem?" Miss Brigid asks.

"No!" Catherine rummages through her bag, pulls her flour baby out from a jumble of shoes and extra clothes, and props it up on a chair. "Sorry! I had to get Meredith. She likes to watch." Catherine races back to her spot as Miss Brigid shakes her head and starts the music.

I don't know these steps yet, but when the music begins, I can't keep my sneakers still. The Novice class is about the same size as ours, but the dancers are more powerful, more sure of themselves, and that makes them a lot louder.

Tick-a-tuck! Tick-a-tuck! Tick-a-tuck! They fly over the floor in unison, arms tight to their sides.

"Good, but I'm not hearing the clicks," Miss Brigid says when the song ends. "Line up and let's do a click exercise."

I tap my sneaker-heels together while the Novice girls kick their way forward.

"Click-two-three, click-two-three . . . Step! Click-down!" Miss Brigid calls. "Much better!"

All the heel clicking reminds me of Dorothy's magic ruby slippers from *The Wizard of Oz*, and that reminds me of my latest wish. "Hey . . . ," I whisper to Dasha. "When do you have another one of those language tests?"

She'd been smiling, watching the dancers, but now her face falls. "Tomorrow." She sighs. "I study all week but . . ." She shrugs as if it's hopeless. I want to tell her it's not, that things will be better this time, but she'll think I'm just being nice. She'll find out soon enough.

"Very nice, ladies!" Miss Brigid calls when the class is over. "Who's going to Montreal?" They all raise their hands. "Great! I'll see you there."

Catherine comes back over to change her shoes. "Are you going this weekend?" I ask.

"Yep. My sister has a gymnastics meet in Vermont Friday night, so we're going up from there and staying in a hotel." She shrugs. "Montreal's a huge feis, though, so I don't really have a chance of top three. I'd need a first place to move up to Prizewinner."

The kids in the Prizewinner class are coming in now. They're mostly high school dancers, but there's one girl who looks like she's about our age. Her mom is dressed in a fancy business suit with high heels. I turn back to Catherine. "Who's that?"

"Leah James," Catherine says. "She's in eighth grade at our school—just moved here from New York City. She used to go to some magnet school there for performing arts. She's amazing. I heard she moved up to Prizewinner when she was like eight."

I watch Leah stretching with one long, muscular leg propped up on a chair and wonder what it would be like to be that good at something.

"See you guys Saturday." Catherine heads for the door.

"You are forgetting your flour!" Dasha calls.

"Shoot!" Catherine runs over, swoops up Meredith from her chair, and leaves. Dasha and I gather up our stuff and head for the door too.

As I walk past Leah, she picks up her dance bag, and

a laminated card falls out and drifts to the floor. It has an ocean scene and a poem or something on it. I bend over to pick it up for her, but she swoops down in front of me and almost knocks me over when she grabs it.

"Sorry," I say.

"It's okay," she says quietly. She doesn't smile; she turns and lines up with the other Prizewinner kids. The music starts, and their feet move so fast I can't even count the clicks. If those hard shoes were ruby slippers, they'd be racking up wishes like crazy.

It's dark by the time I get home, but dinner's not ready yet. I saw on the way home that Drew and Mrs. McNeill are still out fishing, so I pull my snow pants on over my leggings and tug on my boots.

"Where do you think you're going?" Dad asks when he looks up from the stove. "You're not going to miss my garlic-ginger stir-fry, are you?"

"I won't be long. But Drew has his basketball tryouts tomorrow, so I want to wish him luck and maybe fish a little while before dinner, okay? The moon's out, so there's plenty of light. And I'll be back in half an hour."

He looks at the clock on the microwave. "No later, okay? Mom will be back from her book group then."

"Thanks!" I hurry out the door and down to the lake. Mrs. McNeill and Drew are fishing closer to shore tonight, not far from the spot where my fish lives.

"How's the fishing?" I ask when I reach them.

"Meh," Mrs. McNeill says. "We've caught a few."

"Little things," Drew says. "Probably don't even add up to a pound yet." He pats the side of the bucket he's sitting on, and my heart jumps into my throat.

What if they caught the wish fish and didn't hear it talk? What if it doesn't always ask to be let go? What if it only talks to me? Or to people who are alone? What if my fish is in the bucket right now, about to be hauled off to fish-fry land?

"Can I see?" I point to the bucket under Drew's behind.

He looks up at me. "They're just perch." He doesn't get up.

"I know, but . . ." I can't explain that I want to check for emerald eyes and make sure none of them are offering wishes in exchange for freedom. "Can I see, please? One of the fish I caught the other day had a . . . a weird marking. It was small, so I let it go. I'm wondering if you caught the same one."

"Who cares?"

"For goodness' sake, Drew, get your frozen rump off that bucket and let her see," his nana says.

Drew gets up and pries the lid off the bucket. "Happy now?"

I peer into the moonlit bucket of water at three small fish. They're all quiet, with regular beady black fish eyes. "Yeah. Thanks. I don't think it's the same fish."

But a minute after I drop my line in the water, that fish is back on my hook. I'm sitting closer to Drew and Mrs. McNeill this time, so as soon as it asks to be let go and makes the wish offer, I turn away from them. "Let Drew be amazing at tryouts and make the basketball team," I whisper.

"What?" Drew says.

"Nothing." I drop the fish back into the lake and look at my watch. "I should actually go in for dinner. Good luck at tryouts tomorrow!"

"We should call it a night too," Mrs. McNeill tells Drew. "Tomorrow's a big day."

Drew lets out a heaving sigh that's practically long enough to melt the whole lake. "It doesn't matter what I do. I'm doomed." He reels in his line and packs everything onto the sled.

"Maybe not as doomed as you think," I say as we start back toward shore.

"What's that supposed to mean?" Drew says.

"Nothing," I say. The sled scrapes along the frozen snow. Everything's sparkling in the moonlight. "Nothing at all."

Chapter 7

Flying Colors

School drags by on Monday.

I walk by Roberto Sullivan in the hall. He's guarding his flour baby from his friend Josh, who keeps trying to poke it with a sharp number two pencil. Roberto still doesn't know I exist. I hope Drew's wish goes better than this one did.

We have a quiz in math. We work on our self-portraits in art class and play badminton in gym. All we do in Spanish is work on our town drawings. We had to label all the places in Spanish—escuela for school, biblioteca for the library, panadería for the bakery. That took about two minutes, so now everybody's shading in rivers and lawns.

Catherine comes up to my desk before science class starts. She's reclaimed her seat from Bobby O'Sullivan. He's over by the window now, too far away to pass notes, but he still stares at me from across the room. "Hey, are you going to do science fair this year?" Catherine says, balancing her flour baby on her hip. "And do you want to work together?"

"Sure!" Then I think about Dasha. I hope she'll pass her test and be in our science class soon enough to do the fair. "How many can we have in a group?"

"Mrs. Racette said three or four. Maybe Dasha would want to be in our group too? You guys will be moving up to Novice soon, so we could meet at my house on Sunday afternoons before dance."

"Perfect. Drew might be able to help too." Even though Drew said he wasn't doing it, I'm hoping he'll change his mind. "Got any ideas for projects?"

"I've been looking online," Catherine says. "Maybe something with bacteria?"

"Maybe." That sounds cool, but bacteria have a pretty high yuck factor. If I'm not careful, I could end up being known as the "Germinator" or worse. "Let's keep thinking."

When the bell rings, I look for Dasha in the halls, but then I remember she had that language testing today. It always takes a whole morning.

On the way to social studies, I see Leah in the hall with some other eighth graders. It's weird—I must have walked past her a hundred times in this hallway without noticing. Seventh and eighth graders don't mix much. But

Leah's more interesting now that I know what an incredible dancer she is. She sees me looking at her, and I'm afraid that's weird, but she smiles and gives a little wave. I wave back and hurry to class.

We're coloring Thirteen Colonies maps today—red for southern, green for middle, and blue for New England. When I drop my green pencil, Bobby O'Sullivan swoops in and grabs it for me before it even hits the ground.

Finally, class ends, and I find Dasha by our lockers. She gives me a thumbs-up.

"You passed?" I call, even though I knew the fish would take care of things.

"I pass with . . . how did she say it? Flying colors? But I did not use colored pencil. Just regular one."

I laugh. Figures of speech are tough when you're learning English. "The phrase 'flying colors' isn't really about colors," I tell Dasha. "It means you did well, and that's awesome! Now you'll be in more classes with Catherine and me at school *and* at Irish dance!" Which reminds me, "We have to leave for the feis early Saturday morning, okay?"

Dasha nods and does a few jig steps down the hall. I fall into step next to her. Irish dancing in sneakers isn't the same, but it's better than not dancing at all.

When the school day ends, I spot Drew walking toward the gym as if each of his fancy new sneakers weighs about a thousand pounds. I can't wait to see him *after* tryouts.

I volunteer to help put up a "Getting Ready for Pi Day" bulletin board after school so I can hang around until Drew is finished.

At three thirty, I find him at the art club bake sale, counting pennies and trying to negotiate a lower price for his Rice Krispie treat.

"Hey! How'd you do at tryouts?" I ask.

He looks up, surprised. "Good. *Really* good. It was weird." He looks down at the sneakers. "I guess maybe these helped." He shrugs. "I don't think I'll find out if I made the team until tomorrow, though."

"Are you buying that or not?" a girl with a tie-dye scarf asks him. "All prices are firm."

Drew waves the treat at her. "I can't believe you're getting fifty cents for these. It's not even a full-size bar." Then he turns to me. "Do you have a quarter? I'll split it with you."

"That's okay." I hand him a quarter, just as the basketball coach, Mr. Breyette, walks up.

"Got a minute, Drew? I'd like to speak with you in the gym."

"Sure." Drew looks at me. "You fishing later?"

"Yep. See you in a while."

Drew walks off eating his Rice Krispie treat, and I go outside. Mom's car is parked in the pickup circle. She's talking on her cell phone, scowling at whoever's on the other end.

"Really?" she says as I get into the car. "You'd think that sending that tuition check every semester would give me the right to know if she's been to class." Mom glances over at me, then lowers her voice. "All right, then please do that. Thank you." She hangs up. "How was your day?"

"Good," I say as we head for home. "Who was that on the phone?"

"Your sister's school. Abby hasn't been returning our calls—and I'm sure she's fine, but I wanted to double-check and make sure she's been going to her classes and . . ."

"Aw, Mom, leave her alone. She's not ten years old. She's fine."

"Have you heard from her lately?" Mom asks.

"Well, not really." I pull out my phone. My text from a couple of weeks ago is still sitting there unanswered. I guess we've both been busy. "She's probably just got stuff going on."

"I know." Mom sighs again. "Let's hear about your day."

I tell her about the math test and coloring maps and Dasha's language test.

"Got homework?" she asks as we pull into the driveway.

"No. But I'm going out ice fishing with Drew and Mrs. McNeill for a while if that's okay."

"That's fine. You sure conquered your fear of the ice this winter."

"Kind of. Yeah. Anyway, I want to see if I can earn a

little more money before Friday. I can't wait to shop for my solo dress."

I gather up my backpack and lunch box and water bottle and start to get out of the car, but Mom's just sitting there. She takes a deep breath. "I need to talk to you about this weekend."

My heart sinks because I know that tone of voice. It's the I'm-letting-you-down-even-though-I-promised voice. The voice that's already asking me to be grown up about being disappointed, only I can't.

"Mom, no . . ."

"I'm sorry. I found out today that they're sending me to a school health conference in Albany from Friday to Sunday. I've been in this job a week, Charlie. I can't say no. Maybe you could ride with Catherine?"

Any other feis, that would work, but not this one. I shake my head. "They're going straight to Montreal from her sister's gymnastics meet in Vermont Friday night and staying over. What about Dad?"

"Dad has his ski trip."

"Can't he stay home?" Tears are running down my cheeks now because I know the answer's no. Dad has airplane tickets, and his college friend will be there waiting for him, and they can't cancel the whole trip because I have a dance competition.

I get out of the car and stomp toward the house.

Mom follows me. "Charlie, please." Mom puts her purse down on the kitchen table and gets herself a glass of water. "The Albany feis is the first weekend in April, and—"

"That's two whole months from now! Mom, we *promised* Dasha a ride too. If we can't go, we can't move up to the other class. We need to be in Novice with Catherine because we're working on a science fair project together, and we're going to meet on Sundays before dance, and if we can't go to the feis, we can't move up and everything will be messed up. Please? Can't you just . . . ?" But then I stop talking. Because there's no good way to finish that sentence. Mom has to go to the conference for her new job. And Dad can't cancel his trip.

Finally I say, "Can Abby come home and take me?"

"No. She's been struggling with her academics, Charlie. She needs her weekend to study."

"Fine." My eyes sting with tears. I grab my backpack, go to my room, and take out my phone.

Charlie: Hey . . . are you there?

I wait a while. Abby's classes end at noon on Mondays. She should be free.

But she doesn't answer.

Charlie: I REALLY need to talk to you.

I wait some more, hoping the phone will ring, hoping Abby will see my text and understand that I need her. But my words sit there on the screen by themselves.

So I give up on texting and call. Abby's voice mail picks up. "Hey, this is Abby. You know what to do!" It beeps. I hang up and flop down on my bed.

Usually, I love my room with its bright-blue paint and the multicolored handprint border that Abby and I made when I was little. Big red hand, little blue hand, big yellow hand, little purple hand . . .

But today, I'm tired of being the youngest in the family. I hate the way everybody else's plans matter more than mine.

Besides, all those colors remind me of the bright solo dresses I won't get to shop for—blues and oranges, whites and greens and reds—sparkling on the rack with other girls pawing through them. I can't believe I caught all those stupid fish to earn money for my dress. I think of all those afternoons with my toes freezing in my boots and my fingers numb, and now I can't even go.

But then I think of the fish with the emerald eyes.

Chapter 8

The Fifth Wish

Mrs. McNeill's car is at Drew's house just like every day she stays with him after school, but she's not outside. The garage door is closed, and the sled and ice fishing stuff are nowhere to be seen, so I knock on the door.

"Is Drew here?" I ask when she answers.

She shakes her head. "He's gone to the store with his dad to buy some warm-ups for basketball."

"He made the team?" I try to look surprised, even though I knew he would.

Mrs. McNeill smiles one of the biggest smiles I've ever seen from her, and that's saying something. "That boy is full of surprises. Apparently, he did so well at tryouts that he not only made the team but is also going to be on the starting lineup for the first game."

"That's awesome!"

"Isn't it?" she says. "But he won't be around to fish today. I'm going to stay in too. I'm fighting a cold."

"That's okay." I start to leave, but as soon as I turn around, I see Mom's silhouette in the kitchen window and I remember that I need a wish.

"Mrs. McNeill?" I turn back to the house before she closes the door. "Do you think I could borrow a pole and a lure? I'd love to go out for a while this afternoon. It wasn't that cold last night, so I can use one of the old holes. I won't need the auger."

She shakes her head. "Not by yourself. That's rule number one on the ice."

"What if I ask my mom or dad to go with me?"

She raises her eyebrows as if she can't quite picture Mom touching a cold, flopping perch. "Sure, that's fine if they're willing." She nods toward the garage. "There are poles ready to go, leaning in the corner. You can take two, and grab a bucket to share."

"Thanks!" I take the gear from the garage and hurry back to our house.

"Hey, Mom?" I call into the kitchen. "Do you want to go down to the lake for a while?"

"Not now. I should have started on dinner half an hour ago."

"Okay! See you in a while." I duck outside before she can say anything else.

I asked. That's what I told Mrs. McNeill I'd do. I feel a twist of guilt in my chest because I know that's not what she meant, but I need the ice tonight.

I pick up one pole—the lure's still tied on from the other day—and leave the other one and the bucket on shore. I won't be keeping the fish I catch.

The ice is quiet this afternoon—all settled with nothing to say. It's wetter and more slippery than usual, since the sun's been beating down all day. I walk out carefully, sliding one foot ahead of the other until I get to the fishing hole by the point. It's crusted over with the thinnest cover of ice. I give it a poke with the end of my rod, and the ice cracks so a thin layer like broken glass floats on the water's surface. I clear it away, drop my line in the water, and wait.

I stand with my boots in the dusting of snow, waiting for a tug, until my nose starts to run. I forgot to bring Kleenex, so I pull a Drew and wipe it on my sleeve. I'm glad my wish for him worked out.

And I really hope the fish is here today, willing to grant one more wish. I need Abby to come home from college this weekend so she can take me to my feis. Her grades will be okay. One day away from her books won't matter. I'll help her study in the car. I can quiz her on her chemistry vocabulary or whatever. I just want to go to my feis.

I bounce the lure a few feet below the surface. The lake is so quiet today. Maybe I won't get a chance to make a wish at all. The sun sinks behind the trees, and I'm getting ready to reel in my line when I feel a tug. I tug back, and the fish is hooked.

When I bring it up, its eyes are as bright as I remember.

"Please," it says in that gravelly voice. "Release me, and I will grant you a wish."

I ease the fish off the lure and hold it in my hand. I take a breath, ready to wish, and hesitate. This is the first wish that's really only about me. The first one that's truly selfish. At least, it's the first wish like that I've made since I understood the fish was real and I wasn't just messing around. I can't help feeling like those wish-story people who should know better but don't.

The fish twitches in my hand, and inside my chest, my heart does the same thing. I'm afraid of this wish. But I've never wanted anything as much as I want to dance in my new solo dress.

I've worked so hard for it. I spent practically every January afternoon out on the ice. I've been plowing through my homework during lunch and getting up early to finish whatever I don't wrap up before bed. I've been bundling myself up in five thousand layers that still can't keep my hands warm in the lake-wind and hauling buckets of bait out here every day instead of playing with Denver or watching TV or practicing dance on the kitchen floor. I've raised the extra dress money, all on my own. And I need to go to my feis.

I say the words before I can think any more. "Let Abby come home from college for the weekend." And I drop the fish back in the water.

I text Abby that night, but she doesn't answer. That's okay. She'll call soon to let us know she's coming home.

All week, I wait.

"Have you heard from Abby?" I ask Mom after school on Tuesday.

"I left another message yesterday, but she hasn't called back."

"Any word from Abby today?" I ask on Wednesday.

"Not yet," Mom says.

My phone dings with a text right after I get in bed Wednesday night. I jump up to answer, but it's not Abby.

> Hi, Charlie! It's Bobby! Hope it's okay I got your
> number from Catherine! I just wanted to say hi!!!
> <3 <3 <3

I stare at Bobby's words and his less-than-three hearts and his exclamation points.

Wishes are pretty overrated sometimes. I turn off my phone and get back into bed.

By Thursday, I'm starting to think I used up all the magic on my other wishes and the feis just isn't going to happen.

The school day crawls by. The only highlight is when Catherine and three other people show up for science covered in flour. But she has Meredith with her, and Meredith looks fine. "Whose kid busted open?" I ask.

"Roberto Sullivan's," she says, brushing flour off her jeans. "It was awful. He left it in the gym locker room, and some of the other guys took it and started shooting baskets with it. Somebody missed a rebound, and it exploded in a giant cloud of flour-baby."

When I see Roberto in the hall after science, he's covered in flour too. I say hi. He ignores me. And reminds me again that magic doesn't always work.

By dinnertime, I've given up on my Abby-home wish. I'm pushing flakes of salmon around my plate, trying to figure out what I'm going to say to Dasha, when Dad's cell phone rings. He pulls it out of his pocket, frowns at the display, and looks at Mom. "I better take this." He stands up. "Hello?"

"Is it Abby?" Mom mouths at him, but Dad shakes his head. He listens to whoever's on the phone for a long time, then asks, "What do you recommend?"

Mom stares at him, as if by looking hard enough she'll be able to hear the conversation.

Denver nudges my ankle under the table, so I slip him a piece of broccoli. This conversation is going on a long time.

Finally, Dad takes a deep breath and lets it out slowly. "Okay. We'll be there to pick her up tomorrow."

My heart jumps at those words—Abby's coming home!

But then Dad sits down and sighs. "That was the student health center on campus. They're keeping Abby overnight and say she needs to have some tests done."

"Is she having stomach troubles again?" Mom asks, and Dad nods. "Worse than usual?"

"Apparently. She hasn't been able to eat or drink much." Dad looks up at the microwave clock. "I'm going to see if Dr. Porter is on call tonight. It would be great if he could meet us at the hospital tomorrow. And then I better call Tom and tell him I'm not going to make it skiing."

"No, you should go," Mom says, but she sounds stressed out. "I can miss the conference. I'm not going to travel with Abby sick."

Dad shakes his head. "She's been through this before, and she'll be fine. You just started this job. Tom won't mind. He takes solo ski trips all the time. And I'm already off work. I'll take care of it."

He takes his phone into his office while Mom and I clear the table.

I can hear him in there, canceling his flight, then explaining to his college friend why he can't go skiing after all. Bits of conversation drift over the water running in the kitchen. "I need to be there for my daughter," he says. "Family first."

When I hear that, my eyes burn and the plates I'm scrubbing turn all blurry in the sink.

Abby always seems to get Mom's and Dad's attention, whether she's scoring a soccer goal or complaining about stomach cramps. I swallow hard because I hate feeling this way. It's awful and selfish and babyish, but I can't help it. I know Abby's sick and needs to have tests now. I know that's important.

But my feis was important too.

And nobody offered to cancel their plans for me.

Chapter 9

Hospital Secrets

When you're in English class reading stories about wishes, it's easy to see things coming. I remember sitting at my desk, doodling stars in the margins of my notebook, thinking about how stupid all the story-wishers were. Our class had a whole discussion about what we would have done differently if we were the characters, and we were all kinds of smug about it. We would have wished so much smarter than those dumb story-people. Our wishes would have worked out a lot better.

But it's a totally different deal when you're out on the ice with a talking fish flopping between your mittens. When you really, really need something, you forget about using specific language and speaking clearly and not being too greedy and all the other unspoken laws for wishing. You blurt things without thinking. Things like "Let Abby come home from college this weekend," instead of "Let Abby come home from college this weekend. Let there not be anything wrong, and let her be available and happy to take me to the feis." If I were in a story, readers would be rolling their eyes at how dumb my wish was.

But I'm not in a story. And I'm not on my way to the feis. I'm in an emergency room exam room with Abby and Dad, waiting for Abby's nurse to come back.

"I'm thinking of a word," Dad says.

I sigh and look around. "Stethoscope?"

"Nope." Dad looks at Abby. "Your turn."

"This is stupid," Abby says, crossing her arms tight over her chest. She's wearing a bulky UVM sweatshirt over her hospital gown, scowling out from under its green hood. "I need to go home and sleep and I'll be fine."

Dad shakes his head. "The doctor says you're dehydrated and need IV fluids."

Abby shakes her head. "So stupid."

Dad sighs. "The word was tiramisu. It's an Italian dessert. In case anyone was wondering."

The nurse comes back pushing a metal stand with two bags of liquid hanging from it. "I'm going to need you to take off your sweatshirt," she tells Abby.

"It's freezing in here." Abby hugs the thick fabric to her chest and looks at Dad. "Can't I try drinking some water instead? I bet I can keep it down now."

"You can certainly try," the nurse says, "but you need the IV too."

"Seriously? Dad, come on . . ."

Abby can almost always get what she wants from Dad, but this time, he shakes his head. "Doc's orders. But I'll go get you a bottle of water and you can have that too, okay?"

"Thanks." Abby waits until Dad leaves to take off her sweatshirt. The nurse is turned the other way, getting the needle ready so she can start Abby's IV. When she turns back, she takes Abby's hand. Then she stops and stares at the inside of Abby's elbow.

I look there too. Abby has an ugly purple and yellowish bruise. "Geez, Ab. What'd you do to your arm?" I ask.

The nurse glances my way, then looks back at Abby. "It's nothing," Abby says. She pulls her arm back from the nurse and looks down at her hands in her lap. "I was messing around with some weights in the gym at school and dropped one on my arm."

"I need to start your IV now," the nurse says quietly. She looks at Abby, waiting, until Abby gives back her arm. The bruise looks awful, but the nurse finds Abby's vein and gets the IV started. She looks at Abby again. "Do you want to talk with me privately?"

Abby shakes her head. "I want to go home and sleep. Under a blanket." She pulls her sweatshirt over her arms.

The nurse hesitates, then turns toward me. "Would you step outside a minute? I think—"

"She's fine," Abby interrupts. "I don't want to talk. I want to finish and go home."

The nurse sighs. She looks upset that Abby doesn't want to talk about her IV, which is weird. What else is there really to say? The nurse taps the first bag of liquid twice with her fingernail, then leaves and pulls the curtain closed behind her.

Abby turns right to me. "Don't tell Dad about my arm. He'll get on me for being careless."

"He'd be right. You're lucky you only hurt your arm, Ab."

"I know. I usually lift with Olivia and we spot for one another, but she had a sorority thing." She shrugs. "Help me out, okay? I'm not in the mood for a lecture."

Before I can answer, Dad hurries back in with two bottles of water, an orange Gatorade, and a blue energy drink. "What looks good?"

"Just the water, thanks." Abby takes it, unscrews the top, and takes a tiny sip. She looks at me, and her eyes are question marks. I know she's waiting to see if I'll tell Dad about her bruise from weight lifting, but I can't understand why she's so worried. I've always kept Abby's secrets. I'm still the only person who knows she had a crush on Tim Hackett sophomore year of high school. She might not live here anymore now that she's in college, and maybe she's been lame about answering texts lately, but she's still my sister.

When we get home from the hospital Friday night, it's past dinnertime. Abby goes straight to bed. Dad and I order pizza. I'm almost asleep when Mom calls from her conference later, but I can hear Dad telling her Abby's okay, that she seemed much better after they got some fluid in her, that the doctor said she should be able to go back to school in a few days if all goes well. I wait for him to tell Mom what a good sport I was about missing my feis, how I got dragged around the hospital all afternoon and never even complained, but that doesn't come up.

On Saturday morning, I wake up with a treble jig in my head and an angry pit in my stomach. It's 8:50. I should have been up early, on my way to Montreal for the feis, but instead, I slept in.

I should be in my new solo dress by now, camped out on a blanket with Dasha with our dance bags and donuts, maybe practicing a few steps while the Beginners finish their dances. Feiseanna start with lower-level dancers and work their way up to the championship rounds after lunch. So we'd be dancing pretty soon if we were at the feis. Instead, Dasha's running work errands with her father, Dad's out picking up groceries, and I'm staying home "just in case Abby needs anything."

Dasha was nice about it when I told her my parents couldn't take us, but I could tell she was just as disappointed as I was. Now, our next chance to dance at a feis is at the beginning of April. I know it's just two months—sixty boxes on the refrigerator calendar—but it feels forever away.

I pick up my room and read for a while, but even Harry Potter can't keep my attention. I put away the clean clothes Mom left on my dresser, tucking my Irish dance socks into the top drawer. When I clear away the laundry, I see that Mom's left a book of science fair ideas on my dresser. I pick it up, flop down on my bed, and flip through the pages.

Examining the motion of a pendulum.

Boring.

How algae reacts to variations in sunlight.

Who cares?

If we had a more energetic dog, we could do the experiment on the best way to train a pet, with treats or praise. But Denver doesn't perform for treats. He gets all he needs hanging out under the kitchen table.

I close the book and try to think of something else to fill up this crummy Saturday morning, but I can't help looking at the clock.

9:20—Dasha and I would be getting ready to dance now, lining up in front of the stage with our numbers pinned to our dresses. My new dress would be sparkling so much the judges would have to squint.

9:35—We'd be dancing in our soft shoes now—first the slip jig and then the reel.

10:00—We'd be in a break now. They usually have hot chocolate and donuts at the food stands. Dasha and I would be kneeling, leaning over chairs to eat our donuts, keeping the crumbs off our dresses.

10:20—Dasha and I would be waiting by the results wall to see how we did. In Irish dancing, it's all about where you rank compared to the other dancers. I bet we'd each have one first by now.

11:00—We'd be dancing either the hornpipe or the treble jig. I can't remember which, and looking at the schedule on the website would just make the pit in my stomach grow.

12:20—We'd be done dancing now, having what Mom calls "Pricey Feis Food" for lunch. Pizza, probably. The pizza is never good, but we end up laughing and talking our way through lunch, so even crummy pizza tastes okay.

1:15—Dasha and I would have our medals by now. Maybe enough so they'd clink together when we walk. I remember the first time I went to a feis. This girl—she must have been a Novice or Prizewinner—came in first in every one of her dances. She was walking around with all her gold medals clinking together, and I remember thinking, "That's going to be me someday. Someday I'm going to clink too."

But I am not clinking today. I am not tapping or jigging or kicking either. Because Mom is off learning to be a better nurse and Dad's watching some football game and I'm supposed to check in once in a while to see if Abby needs anything. Because Abby matters way more than I possibly could.

My Sunday is even worse than my Saturday. Everybody shows up for dance class wearing their medals and clinking all over the place. *Everybody* includes Catherine's flour baby, which has a silver medal draped over its onesie. It does not include Dasha and me, who are medal-less and quiet.

We're not practicing in hard shoes today, so I can't even stomp out my frustrations.

Stomping in soft shoes is impossible. It's like shouting into a pillow. No one hears you at all.

Chapter 10

All the Wrong Wishes

"So what's the big deal?" Drew says as we pull the sled out to the ice after his basketball practice on Monday. "There's feces all over the place on winter weekends."

I give him a shove. "It's *feiseanna*. And that's true, but most are far away. I can't go to another feis until April now."

"Whatever," Drew says.

"Why are you so grouchy?"

"Because I was *supposed* to be done with basketball. I was *supposed* to get cut and not have to do this anymore. But my fancy sneakers worked some kind of weirdo magic and I ended up acing tryouts. Only now they don't work anymore, and I stink again."

Oh no. Didn't I wish for Drew to be amazing at basketball? Or did I just ask the fish to make him good at tryouts?

Crud. Please don't let this be my fault. "Drew, you probably just had a bad day or something. I bet—"

"Not a bad day. A bad week. A bad *everything*, except for that one stupid hour at tryouts. I started our first game and didn't make a single shot. Coach took me out after ten minutes."

He picks up the auger and starts redrilling a hole that iced over during the weekend.

I stare at him and try to figure out how I can unwish this mess I made.

"Charlie, you okay?" Mrs. McNeill says. "You seem a million miles away."

"How long does basketball season last?" I ask.

She looks over at Drew. "Too long, if you ask me," she whispers. "I talked with his parents about letting him quit, but they say he made a commitment. I suppose it'll be a character builder for him. Ready to fish?" She hands me a pole and helps me drill a new hole in the ice.

It's been so cold the past week that the ice is more than a foot thick now, and a whole ice-fishing village has sprung up in the bay. Some people who spend all day on the ice haul out tiny little houses, called shanties, to sit in. Some are just a few sheets of plywood nailed together, but others are painted, with shingles on the roofs and pickup trucks parked outside.

Finally, Mrs. McNeill's auger makes it through, and

water splashes up onto the ice. "We're not very far out today," I say, lowering my line into the dark hole. I want to fish now and forget about Drew and basketball and the feis where I didn't get to dance. I just need a good day after the crummy weekend I've had. The only good thing about missing the feis is that now I have the rest of the winter to raise more money for my dress.

"Should be all right, but if not, we can go out a bit more." Mrs. McNeill squints toward the island, where the ice has pushed itself up into a ridge. "Though I'm not thrilled with that pressure ridge by our old spot. Those can make the ice so uneven. Years ago, Drew's grandpa tried to drive a four-wheeler over one and found himself dangling by his back wheels, staring into a crack about four feet across."

"Wow! What'd he do?"

"He wasn't alone, thank goodness. His buddies had brought out a couple of two-by-fours in case they got into trouble, so they managed to lift it back onto more solid ice. Still . . ." She shakes her head and looks down at the hole she just drilled. "I think we'll stay close for today."

She sets up pretty close to me—too close, Drew would complain—but I don't mind. When the fish aren't biting, it's hard to sit so long without talking. And I'm thankful for anything that takes my mind off my rotten wishing skills.

"Will you tell me more about Drew's grandpa?" I ask when Mrs. McNeill is set up and sitting on her bucket. "I only met him once, and it was after he was sick. I can't picture him driving four wheelers over the ice." But I know Drew remembers a grandpa from before that. One he says was the coolest, funniest guy in the world.

"We used to have the best time, skating and four wheeling and fishing," Mrs. McNeill says. She pulls her charm necklace out from under her scarf and turns it over and over between her fingers. "We'd bring Drew's mom—that was before she got all lawyery on us and started wearing suits instead of snow pants—and spend pretty much the whole weekend out on the ice." She looks half happy, half sad, remembering.

"When did he get sick?" I ask. There's a little tug on my line, but when I tug back, nothing's there.

"Got a bite?"

I shake my head. "Musta lost it."

She bounces her line and looks out over the whiteness that stretches all the way to the Vermont shore. "Thing is with alcoholics, there's not a day you can point to when everything changes." She sighs, then looks at me. "You knew Drew's grandpa was an alcoholic?"

I shake my head. I didn't.

She nods slowly. "A lot of people didn't know because he went to work and kept his job and seemed fine most of the time, I guess. But he was struggling a long while before he got sick."

"That must have been hard," I say.

"It was. But you get to a point and realize it's out of your control. There's nothing you can do for a person when—oh! Hold on!" She gives her pole a yank, stands up, and reels it in. The line bends more than it usually would, and when she pulls in her fish, it's the biggest one we've caught.

"Woo-hoo! Look at this one!" she calls to Drew, holding it up on the line.

"Think it's more'n four pounds?" he calls over. "I think that's the best they got in the tournament so far."

Mrs. McNeill lifts the fish up and down a few times, testing its weight. "It'll be close." She puts it in the bucket, sits down, and works a new minnow onto her hook. "Anyway," she says. "Yes, it was hard. I was sad a lot because I so wanted to fix him. But then I decided I needed to keep busy. I was still sad, and I made space for that sadness, but I didn't invite it in to take over the house, you know?"

I nod, even though I'm not sure I do.

"There's a prayer that helped me a lot back then. I always mess up the words," she says, "Something like . . . Lord, please give me patience to accept what I cannot change, courage to change what I can, and wisdom to know the difference."

"Can you say that again?" I ask, and she does. "I like that. It's kind of what I'm doing here." I nod at my pole, still quiet in the water. "I can't turn back time and go to the feis that I missed, but I can keep fishing to earn more money for—oh!" I feel a tug on my line then and reel in a medium-sized perch. "It's no four-pounder, but I'll take it."

Mrs. McNeill nods. "Half a dress-crystal there?"

I look at the fish. It's pretty small. "Maybe a tenth of one. But every little fish counts."

I still wish I'd made a better wish so I could have danced in Montreal. But wishing aloud for that sort of thing would probably make a bigger mess, so I keep that one to myself.

I've given up on the idea of wishing away Drew's basketball mess too, even though he hates it and hasn't gotten any better. His dad won't let him quit, but Drew's talking with the coach about maybe doing something else with the team instead of actually handling the ball. He's hoping for a job keeping stats, and maybe his dad will be settle for that. Either way, I've decided that trying to fix Drew's problem with the fish isn't worth the risk of messing up again. With my luck, I'd make some dumb wish and Drew would end up twelve feet tall.

I'm not even trying to catch the wish fish anymore.

The hole in the shallow water by the point freezes over. Sometimes it's hard not to think about that sparkly eyed fish beneath the ice, but mostly, I focus on the bigger fish that can help pay for my dress.

I like Mrs. McNeill's idea about keeping busy, so that's what I do.

I offer to watch Catherine's flour baby after school during drama club because every time she leaves it in one of the auditorium seats to watch the rehearsal, the stage crew hides it from her. They think it's hilarious. But Catherine was late for her trombone lesson once because she had to look for Meredith for twenty minutes before she found her back in the lighting booth. So now I babysit after school every Thursday.

Dasha and I are stuck in the Advanced Beginner dance class for now, but we find online videos and start teaching ourselves the Novice dances. That way we'll be ready when we move up.

There's science fair to think about too. Now that Dasha passed her language test and doesn't have to be in ESL classes anymore, she has science with Catherine and me. We're going to work together; we just have to agree on a project. Catherine found some report from the United Nations that said people ought to consider adding bugs to their diets to help solve the world's food crisis. She thought that would be a cool project, but I'm not sure I'm ready to be called a bug eater for the rest of my life.

I've also kept busy fishing. Mrs. McNeill says this is the best ice season Lake Champlain has seen in twenty-five years.

The last day of February is my best fishing day yet. I pry the lid off my bucket to show Billy, and he whistles. "Those are some beauties. Fish fry tonight!" He hands me a crisp ten dollar bill to add to my savings. That brings my dress fund to five hundred fifty dollars—three hundred from Mom and Dad and two hundred fifty from ice fishing.

We're quiet on the walk home until Drew asks, "Do you know how to escape from an elephant stampede?"

"No idea," his nana says.

"Climb a tree," Drew says. "But if it's a stampede of giraffes, you try to get to water."

"Won't they just wait for you like the killer bees?" I ask.

Drew shakes his head. "Giraffes hate water. Unless they're thirsty and need a drink."

I nod. "Have you found anything in that book about surviving basketball season?"

"Not yet," he says. "But I did get Dad to agree that I don't have to play in games as long as I do something else for the team."

"That's great! Did you get a job keeping stats?"

"Not exactly." Mrs. McNeill's trying not to laugh. "He's going to be the mascot."

"Wait," I say. "The Lakeside Champs' mascot is . . . You're gonna be the lake monster?"

"Yeah. I'm Champ. They got this big fuzzy green costume for me." Drew kicks at some ice at the edge of the sidewalk. "I tried it on today. It's kinda hot and smelly in there, but I guess anything's better than playing. At least nobody boos the lake monster."

"You should come to one of the games, Charlie," Mrs. McNeill says as I turn to head up my driveway.

The thought of Drew dressed up like Champ the lake monster makes me want to laugh, but I'm the one who got him into this whole mess, so that would be pretty mean.

"I'll try to make the next game." I wave and head inside my house. The kitchen smells like roast chicken, and for the first time in days, I'm not stressed out about my fish wishes. Even though I messed up, things are working out okay. I'm helping Dasha with her classes. Drew will be all right as the lake monster, even though he's not thrilled about his smelly costume. And Bobby . . . well, Bobby is still swooning, but he's not all that bad.

"Hey, Mom! Hey, Dad!" They must be upstairs or in the basement doing laundry. I kick off my boots and sit down on the mudroom bench to wiggle out of my snow pants.

Denver trots up to say hi and lick my hands. They probably taste all fishy.

Mom's cell phone rings on the kitchen counter, and I glance down at it. The number has Abby's area code at school. It's not her, but I know I need to get it in case it's the health center and she's sick again.

When I answer, a woman's voice says, "Hello, Mrs. Brennan?"

"No, but hold on. I'll get her." I holler upstairs. "Mom! Phone!"

Mom comes down with a pile of laundry, sets it down, and takes the phone from me. "Hello?" she says, and then listens.

Dad comes downstairs with another basket of clothes and starts for the basement, but Mom holds up her finger for him to stay. For a long time, she listens.

Then she says, "I'm sorry . . . that's . . . that's impossible. Okay . . . okay . . ." She listens for another few minutes. She blinks a lot. Finally, she says, "Okay . . . yes . . . but she'll be all right?" Mom's quiet for a minute then. A tear slides down her cheek. She takes a deep breath. "Okay . . . okay, yes. Thank you very much." She hangs up the phone and looks at Dad. "That was the university health center. They've got Abby."

"Is she okay?"

Mom blinks fast. "Charlie, go up to your room, please."

"Why? Isn't Abby all right?"

"She'll be fine. But Dad and I need to talk. Now go." Mom points, and I go. But I stop at the top of the stairs and squat down to listen.

"What's going on? Is it her stomach again?" Dad says.

"No," Mom says, and even upstairs, I can hear the deep, shaky breath she takes. "They say she's been using heroin."

Chapter 11

Signing the Car

Mom and Dad move into the living room and talk in quieter voices that I can't hear anymore. That's fine, because it's not true anyway.

Abby's not using heroin. She's probably having stomach troubles again, is all, and somebody made a mistake.

We learned about heroin in the D.A.R.E. Program, when Officer Randolph came to talk to all the fifth graders about drugs. We had to watch a movie, and in the heroin part, these raggedy, greasy-haired people were sitting around a smoky room, sticking needles in their arms.

Abby looks nothing like those people. She washes her hair every day and pulls it into a bouncy, curly ponytail.

Abby's an athlete. She takes care of herself. She's smart. She did Model UN and had the second-highest grades in her whole senior class in high school.

Abby doesn't even like to take Advil when she has a headache.

And she signed the car.

Every year when Officer Randolph comes to Thomas Elementary School, he brings the police department's D.A.R.E. car, and all the fifth graders get to sign it in permanent marker as a pledge not to do drugs. Abby signed that car. I saw her name on it when I signed six years later. Abby's name was in purple, her favorite color.

The health center people are wrong.

I go back downstairs and stand in the doorway to the living room. Mom and Dad are on the couch. Mom's elbows are on her knees, and her hands are over her face. Dad's arm is around her. He looks up.

"I heard what they told you," I say. "But Abby would never use drugs."

Mom sits up. Her eyes are puffy and red. She looks at me and takes a breath as if she's about to talk. Then she looks at Dad.

"It's hard for us to believe too," he says.

I shake my head. "Why are they saying that? Just because she has stomach problems—"

"Charlie, listen." Dad reaches out and takes my hand. "Abby's suitemates found her in her dorm room this afternoon. She was having trouble breathing, so they took her to the university health center. Abby told the nurse she'd injected heroin. They say from the bruises on her arm, it's obviously not the first time."

I feel like someone punched me in the stomach. I look at Dad. "She told me those bruises were from lifting weights."

"You saw her arm?"

I nod. "At the hospital. When she was home before." My eyes fill with tears. "She told me not to tell you." Abby lied. She said she didn't want Dad on her case about lifting weights without a spotter when really, her secret was so much bigger and uglier.

And I kept it.

"I'm so sorry." I barely get the words out before I'm crying so hard I can't catch my breath. Mom and Dad wrap me in a hug.

"It's okay," Mom whispers. "We're going to get her help. She's going to be okay."

I wipe my eyes with my sleeve. "Really?"

Dad nods. "She told the truth, Charlie. When her friends took her to the health center, the nurse asked if she had used any illegal drugs. Abby told the truth. That's a very good thing."

"It means that she wants help," Mom adds. Her voice is a little stronger now. She sounds a little more like her school-nurse-get-things-done self. "She gave the health center staff permission to talk with us, and the nurse we spoke with was wonderful. She gave us the name of a treatment center in Vermont."

"Are you going to send Abby there?" I can't imagine my sister locked up somewhere with those people from the video.

"She has to call and admit herself. Technically, Abby's an adult," Mom says, even though I can tell she wants to swoop in and take over. "But the nurse says the center has beds available right now. If Abby calls in the morning, they should be able to admit her on Wednesday." Mom looks at Dad. "We'll need to go with her to deal with insurance and sign papers." She takes a deep breath and looks at her watch. "Do you want to get dinner ready while I call Dr. Porter? I want to see what he knows about this treatment center."

Dad nods and turns to me. "Come set the table, okay?"

I lay out the plates and silverware while Dad heats up the chicken we were supposed to eat an hour ago. Mom comes back with her cell phone. "Dr. Porter says that treatment center is excellent, with a great program and a nice farm setting. He says Abby will do well there." She says this as if we're sending Abby off to summer camp.

Dad nods. "That's good."

Then we eat the quietest dinner in the world.

I finish and start to clear dishes, but Mom takes my

plate. "Try to get some sleep. It's late, and you have school tomorrow."

I go to bed. I try to sleep, but every time I close my eyes, I see Abby in that room of people from the video. She looks scared and lost, like she can't understand how she ended up there.

Neither can I.

All through school on Tuesday, I can't stop thinking about Abby.

In science, Catherine asks me about science fair possibilities. I can't think about potato starch or moon phases, so I just nod. "Let's talk about it later."

At lunch, Bobby O'Sullivan plops down next to me with a big box of chocolate he brought to share. "Hi, Charlie!" He gives me a huge smile and holds up his hand.

"Hey, Bobby." I sigh and give him a limp high five. Bobby's been following me around so much that we sort of made a deal. He's allowed to sit with Dasha and me at lunch as long as he promises not to write me any more dragon notes.

Dasha leans around Bobby to ask what we have for social studies homework. I shrug because I don't remember and can't care about that today.

"What's wrong?" Dasha asks. "You act as if you didn't hear me."

"Have some chocolate," Bobby says, shoving the box in my direction. "Did you notice they're shaped like hearts?"

I push it away. "Sorry, Dasha." I shake my head. "I'm just tired." I don't tell her it's because I was awake all night, imagining my sister in a room full of scary-looking people and smoke and needles. I don't tell anybody. Because saying "my sister has a problem with heroin" is like saying she's a criminal. It makes me feel like a criminal too, even though I haven't done anything wrong.

I don't wait for Dasha after school. I go straight outside. Mom's there in the car. "How was your day?" she asks, like it's any other day. Like we're not waiting to find out if Abby can get into a treatment program for people who break all their elementary school promises and tell their sisters liar-stories about lifting weights to cover it up.

"Good," I say. Because a stupid question deserves a stupid answer.

When we get home, Dad's listening to a message on his phone. "Dr. Porter wants us to call him back."

"Let me get changed and we can conference call, okay?" Mom starts for the stairs, then says over her shoulder to me, "Get started on your homework."

"I wanted to go out fishing with Mrs. McNeill and Drew while it's still light, okay?"

"Sure—be back before dark."

I'm glad she's too busy to argue. All day, I've been crav-
ing the quiet of the ice, the bigness of the frozen lake.

And I keep thinking about the wish fish. I don't know
what I'll do if I catch it today. If I've ever needed a wish,
it's now. Even if it were the last wish in the whole lake, I'd
use it to help Abby if I could. But it feels like this might be
too serious for wishing. Like wishing wrong could be more
dangerous than not wishing at all.

But either way, I want to fish. By the time I get dressed,
Mrs. McNeill and Drew are out on the lake. I run-slide over
the ice to meet them.

"Watch that spot by the dock!" Mrs. McNeill hollers. Her voice bounces off the concrete seawall by shore.
I slosh past the dock and see what she means. It's been
sunny today, and the ice is a little mushy here. But it's fine.
Even with slush on top, the ice must still be more than a
foot thick.

"You need to slow down, Charlie," Mrs. McNeill says
when I slide up to her and reach for a fishing pole. She
catches my wrist and makes me stop to listen. "It's March
first, and we're on the back end of this fishing season now.
Every warm day means a little more melting. That happens
faster near docks and streams."

"Okay," I say, and she lets my hand go. I don't see why
she's worried; the ice is plenty thick.

I sit down on my bucket and drop my line in the water. The fishing's crummy. We get a few bites, but Drew's the only one who manages to bring in a fish. It's the tiniest perch ever. For a second, I think it might be the wish fish with the green eyes, but this fish is even smaller.

"Aw, man! Billy ain't even payin' a nickel for this thing." He throws it back.

"*Isn't*," Mrs. McNeill says. "He isn't paying a nickel."

"Not now, he ain't. I threw it back." Drew laughs and looks over at me. "You getting bites?"

"Not really."

"Let's call it an afternoon," Mrs. McNeill says, and we help her load up the gear. She swings wide around that slushy spot by the dock, and I follow to make her happy, even though it would have been fine to cut across.

When I get home, Dad's car is gone. Mom's in the kitchen making sandwiches. "Good news," she says, spreading mayonnaise on a slice of bread while I sit down at the table. "Abby's being admitted to Forest Hills tomorrow."

"Forest Hills?" It must be the name of the treatment center, but it sounds more like a senior citizens' home in the woods than a building full of drug addicts. "Are you taking the day off to drive her there?"

"Dad and I both are," she says, and something twists

in my gut. They have all kinds of time now that it's Abby who needs something. I know this has nothing to do with my feis—this is bad and serious and totally different—but I can't help feeling a twinge of jealousy. Everything feels so messed up.

"Well, that's nice," I say. Denver pads across the floor and sniffs at Mom's sandwiches. She shoos him away, so he comes over to me for some love. Dogs are so much better than people sometimes.

"It's a pretty drive, and we'll only be there about half an hour to fill out paperwork and say good-bye," Mom says. "Do you want to come with us?"

"Are you kidding? I don't want to see those people." The words are out of my mouth before I can think. I was picturing the people from the video. But we're not talking about them. We're talking about Abby. "I mean . . . sorry. It's so weird."

"It's okay," Mom says, slicing a turkey sandwich in half. She blinks, and a tear falls onto the bread. "I understand. Believe me, I do." She shakes her head. "I never thought I'd be in a place like this, but here we are." She wipes her cheek with the palm of her hand and goes back to cutting sandwiches. She arranges them on a plate and sets it in the middle of the table.

Mom's so careful about everything, so careful about taking care of us. What's happening with Abby feels impossible.

You'd think the school nurse would be able to keep her own kid away from heroin.

Ever since Mom found out about Abby, she's been on her computer, looking up things about addiction and treatment and how to get your insurance to pay for it. Before school this morning, I saw her reading a website about why teenagers use drugs, as if she could figure out what she did wrong to make this happen. As if there would be a how-to solution like the directions for fending off a shark in Drew's survival guide.

But there's no answer for this one. Mom didn't do anything wrong.

It's not fair. Life has rules, and if you follow them, things are supposed to work out.

If you place in all your dances, you get to move up to the next level.

If you brush your teeth, you're not supposed to get cavities.

If you love your kids and take care of them and send them to a good college, they're not supposed to stick needles in their arms.

But I guess it doesn't work that way. None of this is working the way it should. Because Abby was stupid enough to try drugs.

"You know what?" I say. "I think I will go with you tomorrow."

Mom nods and hands me a pile of napkins for the table. "I think that would be nice. She'll be in at least two weeks. Maybe more, if insurance covers it. You'll want to wish her well."

"Sure." There are some other things I want to say to my sister too.

Chapter 12

Another Abby

All the way to Vermont, I talk to Abby in my head, practicing what I'm going to say when we pick her up at school.

You wrote your name on the D.A.R.E. car. You promised.

You lied to me at the hospital.

How could you do this to our family?

But when Dad parks the car and we walk into the university health center, the girl who stands up to greet us isn't Abby. Not our Abby anyway.

Her face is grayish. Her hair is matted like she just woke up, and her eyes look so, so tired. Mom sucks in her breath, then rushes up and pulls Abby into a hug. Abby's arms look weak. She's barely hugging back, but she closes her eyes tight and starts shaking with sobs.

It's like I'm watching a TV show with one of those hospital scenes. Like I'm watching strangers. This girl with the scared, washed-out eyes is nothing like my sister.

Dad talks with the health center nurse for a few minutes, and then we all walk to the car. Abby barely looks at me. That's okay. All of the things I wanted to tell her are gone. This other Abby looks so fragile. It feels like saying those things might be enough to make her crumble right down to the sidewalk.

We stop at Abby's dorm to get her stuff. Then it's an hour to the treatment center. Abby spends the whole ride with her legs tucked to her chest, arms hugging them, eyes staring out the window at the dirty snow piled on the side of the road.

I look at her until I can't look at her anymore. Then I take out my phone and scroll through our texts.

Abby: How was yr 1st day of school?

Charlie: Pretty good—thanks! But I might try to switch science teachers. I heard Mrs. Racette is better than Mr. Lamana.

Abby: OMG you have him?

Charlie: Yeah, did you?

Abby: Yes and you totally need to switch. Mr. Lamana's room always stinks. Not sure if it's chemistry mistakes or if he just passes gas in there all day. Make your escape now while you still can!

Charlie: LOL. Do I just go to guidance and ask or what?

Abby: Yep—go see Ms. Santella and she'll hook you up.

I want my sister back. I want the sister who answered me when I needed advice and played the word game with us from across the lake. I want the sister who cared about how my classes were going and cheered for me, even when she couldn't come to my feis . . .

> **Abby:** Hey!! Are you back? How'd it go?
> **Charlie:** On the way home now. I got TWO medals!!
> **Abby:** !!!!!!!!!
> **Charlie:** Thanks! I am soooo excited!
> **Abby:** That is awesome!! Congrats, Riverdance girl!

I want the sister who was healthy and smart and funny and happy.

> **Abby:** Happy Halloween, Charlie!
> **Charlie:** You too! Are you dressing up? Do you still do
>   that in college?
> **Abby:** Totally. My friends and I are going to a party
>   tonight dressed as caffeine.
> **Charlie:** Like . . . cups of coffee?
> **Abby:** Nope! This is what science-geek costumes look
>   like . . .

She sent a picture of four girls wearing black leggings and sweatshirts with letters on them. One shirt's lettering said C_8, one said H_{10}, one said N_4, and Abby's said O_2. I guess that's the chemical symbol for a caffeine molecule. They were all smiling and laughing, Abby most of all.

But that Abby isn't here. The sister beside me in the back seat is broken. Quiet tears run down her face as the car bumps along over potholes on the road to the treatment center. I reach out for Abby's hand, but she pulls it back and keeps staring out the window.

Dad almost drives right past the place, probably because it's nothing like a hospital or clinic. Forest Hills looks like any Vermont farm tucked into the foothills of the Green Mountains. There are two white farmhouse-type buildings, plus an enormous barn. Half of it is weathered and old, with peeling paint and chickens strutting around the door, but the other half looks brand new.

Dad parks in front of the new part of the building near a door that says Reception. He lifts Abby's duffel bag and suitcase from the trunk.

A goat comes over and tries to take a bite of the duffel bag strap. Dad shoos it away. "Boy, the counselors here sure are pushy."

Abby smiles, but it's not her real smile. She's looking at a sign over the reception door.

YOU ARE NO LONGER ALONE.

Abby blinks fast. Two tears slip down her cheek, and I wonder why that sign made her cry. The heroin people in the D.A.R.E. video were never alone—they were always in crowded rooms. But their eyes looked lonely. I guess Abby's do too.

Dad closes the trunk. Mom steps up behind Abby and puts a hand on her back. "Ready?"

Abby swipes at her eyes with her jacket sleeve. She nods, and we go inside.

The reception room is just a big living room—couches, chairs, and bookshelves—along with a simple wooden desk. The woman sitting at it stands up when we come in. "You must be Abby Brennan." She smiles, reaches out, and shakes Abby's hand as if Abby were a candidate for a job or a customer opening a bank account instead of someone in trouble for using drugs. "It's great to meet you. We have some paperwork to take care of first. Then you can say good-bye to your family, and we'll have you meet with the nurses for your initial screening. While you're with them, we'll search your bags." She looks down at Abby's duffel bag and suitcase. "You know there are no weapons, no drugs or alcohol—that includes personal items like mouthwash with alcohol—no clothing that advertises drugs or alcohol, and no electronics."

Abby nods along with every "no" except the last one. She puts her hand on her back pocket. "That doesn't include phones, does it?"

The woman nods and gives Abby a kind smile. "But we

have phones here, and you're welcome to use them during any of your breaks."

"We'll take it home for you, Ab," Dad says.

Abby sighs, but she gives Dad her cell phone and answers all the woman's questions. Mom and Dad fill out paperwork about insurance and emergency contacts. I sit and listen while they talk about the kinds of treatment Abby will get: group and individual counseling, skills for staying away from drugs, mindfulness training, and acutherapy, which is like acupuncture, I guess. I'm only half listening until the lady talks about giving Abby some drug called suboxone.

"Aren't you supposed to get her *off* drugs?" I say.

"Charlie," Mom whispers. "Be polite."

But the admissions counselor turns to me and smiles. "You're a good sister, asking these questions. But when a person is addicted to heroin and stops using it, she goes through something called withdrawal. Do you know what that is?"

I nod. But really all I know is what we learned at D.A.R.E.—it's some bad thing that happens after you use drugs. "Actually, not really."

"Drugs like heroin actually change the way the brain is wired. Heroin *makes* a person need more heroin. So when someone decides to break free of that, like Abby's doing, the body takes time to adjust. The drug we're giving her will help that to happen more gradually," she says. She looks at Mom, Dad, and Abby then too. "I'm not going to lie to you. Even with the suboxone taper, it's going to be a pretty awful week."

Mom puts a hand on Abby's knee. "You can get through this. We believe in you."

The counselor turns back to me. "Any other questions?"

I have lots. How come Abby can't keep her phone? Why are there so many different parts of the treatment? What if none of it works?

But most of my questions are about how somebody as smart as Abby could be stupid enough to do this, to be here. And then I'm angry all over again.

I walk away, sit down on a couch across the room, open a magazine, and pretend that "Five Ways to Sneak Vegetables into Your Family's Dessert" is the greatest thing I've ever read. But seriously? A person would *have* to be on drugs not to notice that their brownies were full of kale.

I feel a rush of cold wind when the treatment center door opens. I look up as a man and woman walk in holding hands and sink down on a couch. They're younger than Mom and Dad, and they both look sad and tired. I sneak glances at them over my magazine, wondering which one has the problem and what drug it is until the lady's eyes meet mine. Then I realize she's probably wondering all the same things about me.

I look away fast, and a framed photo on the wall catches my eye. It's an ocean scene with writing across the waves. And because anything is better than sitting here looking back at the people looking at me and wondering if I'm on drugs, I get up and walk over to read it.

God grant me the serenity to accept the things I cannot change;

Courage to change the things I can;

And wisdom to know the difference.

At first, I can't figure out why it sounds familiar, but then I realize it's that prayer Drew's nana talked about, the one that helped her when her husband was an alcoholic and she wanted to fix everything but she couldn't. I've seen the photograph before too—on that card that fell out of Leah's dance bag that day.

I glance over my shoulder, but those people are still there, so I turn back and read the prayer-thing again. The trouble with it is that when you're a kid, almost everything falls into that second category of stuff you can't change. Not only Abby but the feis and Drew's basketball mess and Dasha's school problems and everything. You'd think finding a magic fish that grants wishes would help, but it doesn't, because it turns out you're really crummy at wishing.

My phone dings with a text from Bobby O'Sullivan, as if to confirm this.

Hi, Charlie! It's Bobby again! What's up?? <3 <3

Nothing good, Bobby.

I shove my phone in my pocket and rewrite the poster in my head. *God grant me the wisdom to enunciate my wishes, explain them clearly, and stop messing everything up.*

I'm still staring at the dumb poster when Mom puts a hand on my shoulder. "Charlie? We've finished the paperwork. Abby has to meet with her nurses, so it's time to say good-bye."

I walk up to Abby. She looks down at her shoes. She has on her purple ballet flats—the ones she'd never let me borrow because she loved them so much and was worried I'd get them muddy or something. They're all scuffed up and stained now.

"Well," I say. And then I don't know what to say because I'm still angry at her for making us come here, but I can't say that in front of Mom and Dad and the cheery admissions counselor. What *are* you supposed to say when you drop your sister off at a drug treatment center? *Good luck?* That makes it sound like she's here to try out for a play. *Feel better? Just say no?*

There's nothing right, so I just say, "Bye, Abby." I lean in and give her a super-fast hug. "I'm going to wait outside, okay?" I'm halfway out before I hear Mom answer, "Sure, we'll be right there."

She and Dad come out a minute later, both with red, teary eyes.

Dad takes a deep breath as we walk to the car. "I'm thinking of a word," he says.

Mom just looks at him. "Seriously?" She shakes her head, pulls open the car door so hard the chickens scatter, and gets in.

Dad and I put on our seat belts. He backs us out of the parking space. "Sorry," he says quietly. "I thought it might help."

"You thought wrong." Mom twists in her seat and looks back at Forest Hills as we drive down the long driveway. I turn to look too. The goat is chewing on something as it watches us leave. The chickens are heading back to the barn. Somewhere inside, Abby is getting her pulse and blood pressure taken, and a stranger is going through her stuff.

Dad turns on the radio. "The word was sunbeam," he says. "Just in case anybody was wondering."

Chapter 13

Photos and Fortunes

When we get home, Mom orders Chinese food and collapses into a chair at the kitchen table. Denver licks her hand until she gives him a halfhearted pat on the head.

Dad pours two glasses of iced tea and sits down beside Mom. "Go start your homework, Charlie. We'll call you when the food gets here."

I go upstairs, but I don't go to my room. I go to Abby's and sit down on her canopy bed. She got a new green comforter for college, so her old sunflower one is still here. I trace petals with my finger and look at the high school pictures she has pinned to her bulletin board. Abby, Kalisa, and Zoya in their soccer uniforms, their faces painted blue and white for spirit week right before her team won the state championship. Abby and Mrs. Joyner, her favorite teacher, after Abby won the local arts center contest for high school poets. Abby at the beach with Mom and Dad and me, smiling in her new orange bikini.

That was on our family vacation to Maine last summer, the one we almost didn't take because we were trying to save money, but Mom and Dad decided it was important because Abby was getting older and might not want to spend next summer at home. She might have classes or an internship, or maybe she'd want to do a summer study-abroad program.

Or she might be locked up in a treatment center with a bunch of drug addicts and goats. You never know.

In the photo, the four of us are standing at the edge of the waves, laughing because this goofy guy Dad recruited to take the photo shouted, "Say pumpernickel!" instead of "Say cheese!" There's a big brown splotch on my pink T-shirt. I remember . . . I'd been eating my ice cream cone on the boardwalk, licking like crazy because it was so hot, when Abby said, "I'm thinking of a word."

"Sunscreen?" Mom guessed.

"No," Dad said. "I bet it's maverick."

"Igloo," I said, licking around the edges of my cone.

"Nope," Abby said. "Slobber." She pointed to my T-shirt, and we all laughed. We laughed so much that day.

But that was the old Abby. The one who signed the D.A.R.E. car.

I decide that's the Abby I'm going to keep. I reach up,

take the beach picture from the bulletin board, go back to my room, and tape it up over my desk.

I find my math homework—Mrs. Ringold emailed me the assignment for tomorrow—and start factoring the equation in the first question. But I keep looking up at the picture.

I can't understand how this happened.

Mom and Dad are good parents. They never forgot Abby in the car or left her alone in the bathroom to be kidnapped and held for ransom. They cheered at Abby's soccer games and helped with her calculus homework and made her tuna sandwiches with cucumber slices for lunch every day.

The more I think about it, the more I want to cry. And then I'm so mad I could rip that picture in half.

I have homework. I have a science worksheet to do and an English essay to start. We're supposed to meet Sunday to start on science fair stuff, and we haven't even agreed on a topic yet. I need to study my Spanish vocabulary, and I'm not even through my first math problem, and it's all because of Abby.

I take the picture down and hold it for a few seconds. Then I put it in my bottom desk drawer. Abby's smile shines up from among the paper clips and pens, and it makes me even angrier.

None of this should be my problem. Abby brought it all on herself.

And she's getting help, anyway. Those drug treatment center people are taking care of her, and I shouldn't have to worry about it.

I close the drawer and go back to my math.

At dinner, I tell Mom and Dad about the science lab we're doing this week, extracting DNA from a strawberry. I tell them about the extra credit Mrs. Ringold said she'd give us if we find examples of math in the newspaper, and I tell them about Catherine's idea that we study entomophagy— that's the fancy name for eating bugs—for the science fair. I talk through the wonton soup and the sesame chicken and right up to the fortune cookies.

Dad reads his first. *"You will open doors with your charm and patience."* He looks at Mom and makes a funny face with his eyebrows all wiggly.

"So charming," she says, rolling her eyes, but she laughs a little.

"I'll go next." I break my cookie in half and pull out the tiny slip of fortune. *"The man who waits for tomorrow misses the opportunities of today.* What's that supposed to mean?"

"That you should stop procrastinating and finish your homework. I'll get these." Mom starts clearing the table.

"What about yours?" I hand her the last cookie.

She opens it and reads, *"When hungry, order more Chinese food."* She squints at the paper. "And it has the number for Silver Dragon."

"Ha! I'm thinking of a word," I say.

"I've got this," Dad says. "Ventriloquist!"

"Nope."

"Kerfuffle," Mom says.

"Cool word, but nope." I wave Mom's fortune in the air. "Scam."

After I finish my homework, I read an online article about bugs being served in some fancy restaurants. Deep-fried crickets actually sound like they might be okay. Then I take a shower and go to bed. I manage to sleep through the night, and my new don't-think-about-Abby policy carries me through breakfast and out the door to school.

I'm super focused in my morning classes and have my hand up for pretty much every question, so much that Mrs. Ringold says, "You're on top of things today."

On my way to lunch, I make a mental list of things to talk to Dasha about so she doesn't ask me what's wrong again. I want to see what she thinks about the entomophagy idea. I'm going to tell her about Mom's Chinese food fortune-slash-commercial and how I've been ice fishing with Drew and Mrs. McNeill. I want to talk about the feis on April second too.

Dasha's usually late because her locker jams, so I open my lunch box and pull out my fruit snacks.

Bobby O'Sullivan plops down next to me with cafeteria pizza, a goofy smile, and his usual high five. "Hi, Charlie! I'm so, so sorry, but I can't talk much today because I forgot to do my tech worksheet that's due next period. I promise to make it up to you tomorrow. Maybe I'll write you another app!"

"That's totally okay, Bobby." I say a silent thank-you to Miss Grummond for assigning tech homework.

Finally, Dasha pulls out the chair next to mine and sits down.

"Hey! How's your day been?" I hold out my pretzels because we always share, but Dasha shakes her head. She looks upset, so now I'm the one asking. "What's wrong?"

"I did so well on the test. I thought I was ready for my new classes, but . . ." She shakes her head. "Everything goes by so fast," she says, and a tear rolls down her cheek.

"Aw, you'll get it, Dasha. You wouldn't have passed the test if you weren't ready," I say. But as soon as the words are out of my mouth, I remember the words of my wish—*Let Dasha pass her language test*—and my heart sinks. It's the same thing that happened to Drew with his basketball tryouts. I wished her through the test, but now she's left on her own.

Dasha shakes her head. "I'm just not smart enough. I don't think I can do it," she says.

"Yes you can!" I say. And I know that's true. This part isn't like Drew and basketball. He's always been terrible at sports. But Dasha can do this. She's smart. She doesn't need magic. She just needs time. And maybe a little help. "We can work on homework together until you feel better about the language stuff, okay?"

Dasha sighs, but then she nods. "That would help so much. You're a good friend, Charlie," she says, and turns to get her lunch out of her backpack.

That makes my eyes burn with tears. Because I'm a terrible friend who wished her into this mess. But I can't tell her that, any more than I can tell her why I've been so quiet lately, so worried about Abby. I look down and take out my sandwich, but I'm too full of secrets to eat.

"I wonder what we're doing in dance this week?" Dasha asks, unwrapping the pampushka her dad packed for her. She offers me a piece, and I take it. It's like the buns Mom makes for Thanksgiving, but more garlicky.

"We'll probably do treble jig again," I say, happy to talk about something other than wishes.

"I hope we work on hornpipe too. I always mess up this one part . . ." Dasha stands up to show me, and pretty soon we're both stomping and kicking in our sneakers. It's not noisy, but the cafeteria monitor comes over anyway and makes us sit down.

"That's okay," I say. "There's always the seated version." I look under the table and make my feet do the dance moves until Dasha joins in. Then Bobby finishes his tech homework and starts tapping his feet around too. Only he has these huge orange Nikes and knows exactly zero steps of Irish dance.

"You might need a lesson or two," Dasha tells him.

"Maybe Charlie can teach me!" Bobby says, and thumps his giant sneakers around some more. It's so funny that Dasha and I give up our regular dance steps for Bobby's moves. Pretty soon we're all thumping and laughing until our stomachs hurt.

When the bell rings for our next class, we catch our breath and gather our things. Dasha leans over and gives me a hard, fast hug. "Thanks," she says. "I needed to laugh today."

"Me too," I say. It's true. Even though I still haven't told her why.

If you focus really hard on doing math and talking about science projects and hitting the volleyball over the net in gym, you can forget just about anything.

Fishing helps too. It used to be the stomping, kicking rhythm of Irish dancing that took my mind off my problems and tired me out so they didn't matter. But somehow, even though it's all about being still instead of moving, the ice gives me that same sense of worn-out calm.

It's so quiet on the frozen lake—and so pretty. I can't believe I used to be afraid to go out there. It feels like another home now. One where nobody's waiting for the phone to ring from the treatment center.

We head out on the ice first thing Saturday morning. Mrs. McNeill is whistling as she pulls the sled, but Drew has a scowl on his face.

"What's your problem today?" I ask.

"Champ," he says, kicking at the snow.

"He's all grumpy-pants because he found out he has to wear tights with his lake monster costume," Mrs. McNeill says.

The word "grumpy-pants" makes me laugh, but when I see the look on Drew's face, I swallow hard and do my best not to smile. "I bet the costume looks cool."

"How would you like to be a boy jumping around in green tights in front of the basketball team?" He takes the auger and stomps off to drill himself a fishing hole.

Mrs. McNeill shakes her head. "At least he doesn't have to shoot any more baskets." She watches Drew, who's apparently forgotten about fishing and is just drilling holes now, one after the other. "That's enough! You're going to burn out my auger!"

Drew sighs a big gust of a sigh and puts down the

auger. I feel guilty all over again about my fish-wish that made his basketball stress even worse. So I change the subject.

"Hey, Drew, have you thought any more about the science fair?"

"Nope."

"Because Catherine and Dasha and I are researching entomophagy. That's eating insects for food."

Drew forgets to be grouchy for a second. "What kind of insects?"

"Crickets and grasshoppers and mealworms, mostly. I guess they have a lot of protein."

"That's awesome! I bet the exoskeletons are all crunchy. We could serve samples at the science fair!"

"Gross. But also cool," I say. "So are you in?"

"Yeah!" he says, starting to bait his hook. "I bet grasshoppers are awesome dipped in chocolate."

"Everything's awesome dipped in chocolate," I say.

Drew looks up. "Really? What about cockroaches? Or maggots? Or boogers? Or . . ."

"You win." I laugh. "Not everything."

Mrs. McNeill and I get our poles ready too. We each choose one of Drew's fifteen holes and drop our lines in. The sun's sticking around a little longer now that it's March, so we have more time to fish. Today's seven pounds of perch earn me another fourteen dollars when I turn them over to

Billy, and that brings my dress fund to five hundred ninety dollars.

When I get home. Mom and Dad are at the door with their winter jackets on. "You didn't forget pizza and bowling night, did you?" Dad says.

"Oh! No," I say, even though I did. I've been so busy not thinking about Abby that I guess I forgot our plans for the night too. And I'm a little surprised we're still going, with everything that's been happening. But I'm glad.

The pizza at Alberto's has a crispy crust and gooey cheese. The bowling alley is loud in the same great way that Irish dancing is loud—with lots of activity and big booms and a few flying pins thrown in too. Mom and Dad aren't on their phones or computers or talking about Abby. We talk about ice fishing and what kind of dress I want to get, and they cheer when I get two strikes in a row. It's a perfect night, until I ask about our plans for Sunday.

"Can we go to the office store tomorrow morning? I need stuff for science fair. We're going to do that insect project, so we're all meeting at Catherine's house before dance. Dasha and I have to leave early because our class is first, but we'll have time to start on a poster."

Mom looks at Dad. Then she looks at me. "Tomorrow is visiting day at Forest Hills."

"But I have dance. And homework. And I need to work on that science project. We agreed to meet Sunday afternoon." I try to keep talking so they can't say anything, so I won't have to think about Abby and heroin and farm-houses full of chickens and drug addicts. But Dad puts a hand on my shoulder.

"Abby needs our support, Charlie." He looks at me over his glasses. "You can have friends over next week to work on your project. But we're going to Vermont tomorrow. We're going to sit in on one of her meetings and have brunch. As a family."

Chapter 14

Visiting Day

The chickens scatter when we pull into the parking area at Forest Hills, but the goat comes running over to the car, probably looking for Abby's duffel bag again.

"Go on," Mom says, shooing it with her hand as it tries to take a bite of her purse.

"Sedgewick!" a guy in a green jacket hollers from the barn. He jogs over in his work boots, pulls the goat away from Mom, and tries to wipe the slobber off her handbag. "Sorry about that." He smiles at Mom, and his green eyes sparkle. He looks like a film star playing a farmer in a movie.

"That's all right," Mom says. "It's great that this is still a working farm. Do you take care of the animals?"

"I'm actually a counselor," he says, giving Sedgewick the goat a scratch on his head, "but we all wear lots of hats around here, so being a drug counselor also means being a goat herder and chicken wrangler." He looks at his watch. "I'd better finish my work and get cleaned up for our meeting. Enjoy visiting day."

He hurries back to the barn with Sedgewick, and Mom, Dad, and I go to the reception area where we dropped Abby off on Wednesday. It's busier today, full of moms and dads and husbands and wives, I guess. You can tell the patients from the visitors because the guests are all wearing winter coats and boots. The people who stay here are just dressed in their regular clothes. Abby's in jeans and a bright-green sweater. I see her before Mom and Dad, but I don't know what to say, so I just wave.

"Hi." She comes over and hugs Mom first, then Dad, then me. Then she takes a deep breath and sighs.

"How're you doing?" Dad asks.

Abby shrugs. "Okay. Thursday and Friday were awful, but I'm starting to feel a little better. I slept some last night."

"Well, that's good." Mom looks around the room at all the people. "Have you made any . . . friends?" The way she says it I'm not sure if she's hoping Abby will say yes or no.

Abby shrugs again. "You're kind of friends with everybody here, I guess. We have group therapy every day, so you get to know people fast." Abby turns to me. "How's school?"

"Good." I feel like I should say more. I've wanted to talk with Abby for so long, but it feels weird now. How could she care about entomophagy or math equations or Bobby O'Sullivan's love apps when she's stuck in here?

"How's dance?" Abby asks.

"Good."

The movie-star goat wrangler hurries in from outside and saves me from trying to figure out what else to say. "Hey, everyone!" he calls as he's taking off his coat. "If you'd like to join us for an open AA meeting, we're going to be in the conference room down the hall. Plenty of room, and this is an open meeting, so everyone's welcome."

I look at Mom. "What's AA?"

Abby answers instead. "Alcoholics Anonymous. But it's a program for anyone with an addiction problem. We had a meeting Thursday night, and it's pretty good. People talk about their issues." She glances at me, then back at Mom and Dad. "People's kids and siblings come to the open meetings, so everyone's careful what they share. It won't be the detailed, awful stuff we hear in group." She hesitates. "Do you want to come?"

"Of course," Dad says at the same time I say, "No thanks." Mom doesn't say anything aloud, but she gives me a look that says plenty.

You're coming too.

Don't even think about arguing.

Abby needs our support.

So I follow them down the hall and take a seat in a folding metal chair. Abby sits between Mom and Dad, and I sit on Dad's other side with an empty chair next to me. I put my coat on it, but pretty soon the room fills in and there are no more open chairs.

A lady about Mom's age steps up beside the chair and looks down at my coat. "Do you mind if I sit here?" she asks, smiling.

"No, go ahead." I pull my coat into my lap, relieved that I'm sitting by another mom instead of one of the shadier-looking people here. There are a few that really do look like the addicts in those D.A.R.E. videos. There's a guy with bad skin and a too-long beard sitting across the circle from me. Two chairs down from him is a girl with snarly long black hair and a sunken face. She looks barely older than me, even though I'm pretty sure you have to be eighteen to come here. A woman who must be her mom is sitting next to her, wearing a nice wool skirt and tall brown boots. You'd never guess they were from the same family if the woman didn't have her arm around the girl's skinny shoulders.

The other people in the circle look pretty normal. There are two girls and a guy about Abby's age, a handful of people who are probably in their twenties, and one older man who keeps picking at a scab on his chin. He's sitting by a worried-looking woman who hasn't taken off her winter jacket. Some of the younger people are sitting with parents, like Abby is, but others are on their own. I look at the woman next to me and wonder whose mom she is.

The movie-star goat wrangler pulls up a chair, sits down, and says, "Hi, everyone. I'm Jason, and I'm an addict."

I think I must have heard wrong—because didn't he say he was one of the counselors? I'm leaning over to ask Dad when almost everyone in the room calls out, "Hi, Jason!" They say it all together as if they practiced it before we got here.

I stare at Jason while he welcomes everybody and reads some stuff about Alcoholics Anonymous from a big book. Then somebody else reads other stuff about traditions and rules. The words swirl around the room like dust in the winter sunlight coming through the window because I'm still staring at Jason, the movie-star-goat-wrangler-counselor-drug-addict and wondering how somebody who has the same problem as Abby is supposed to help her.

I look over at Mom and Dad and Abby a few times, but they're sitting and listening as if all this is normal.

Then Jason introduces Kali, who looks a little older than Abby. She's wearing skinny jeans and cool purple sneakers. She starts her talk the same way: "Hi, my name is Kali, and I'm an addict."

"Hi, Kali!" everyone says. This time, I hear Dad say it too.

"I'm going to tell you how I ended up here for the third time," she says, and starts talking about her childhood growing up in Brooklyn. I miss most of it because I'm think-ing, *The third time? Why would somebody be here a third time when it's supposed to work the first time?*

Kali tells us all how she loved horseback riding, how she got thrown from her horse and took pain meds while she was recovering. She tells us how she depended on those pills, how she needed more and more of them to feel okay, and it got worse from there. She says it all in this matter-of-fact voice, like she's talking about how she made herself a peanut butter and jelly sandwich instead of how she met scary strangers in parking lots to buy little waxed paper bags full of powder.

Little waxed paper bags full of powder.

I look over at Abby, and what I see is not Abby-today but Abby of winter break, when she took me to dance class, when I found that little bag on her car seat and thought she'd been to the bakery.

Did you get cinnamon donuts without me?

No, that's Seth's.

Who's Seth?

One of the cooks. You should see how high he can throw the pizza dough and still catch it.

And then I'd imagined Seth and his pizza dough and I'd run off to dance class and forgotten all about the little bag that wasn't full of cinnamon and sugar at all.

My chest gets tight. I stare at Abby and wonder what else she lied about.

Then the woman next to me—the one who is supposed to be somebody's mom—starts talking. "Hi, I'm Carolyn, and I'm an addict."

"Hi, Carolyn!" everyone says, as if they're meeting her at a bake sale and not in a room full of liars who ruin everything for their families. And that is about all of the fakeness I can take.

"I have to go," I whisper to Dad. "I'll meet you in the lobby." I push my chair back and walk out the door and down the hallway. I walk through the lobby and outside because tears are streaming down my face, and I can't breathe in this place anymore.

The goat comes running up to me. I push him away and sit down on a wooden bench outside the barn. It's freezing out here, and my jacket is still on my chair next to Carolyn, the addict disguised as a mom.

The goat walks up and stands in front of me.

"What?" I say. "Are you an addict too? Go on . . . Hello, my name is Sedgewick . . ."

He lifts his head and nibbles the fringe of my scarf. He's obviously addicted to chewing other people's stuff. I tug my scarf out from between his teeth just as a minivan pulls into a parking lot. When the driver gets out, Sedgewick runs up to her.

"Careful," I call over. "He likes to eat clothes."

"Thanks for the warning," she says, and laughs. I'm

trying to figure out why she looks familiar when she turns to the passenger's seat. "Come on, Leah. We've missed the meeting, but we can still have brunch with her."

When Leah gets out of the van, I know where I've seen her mom. At dance class, picking up her daughter.

"Hey," Leah says. She gives me a weak wave and looks down.

"Oh. Hi." I stand up from the bench but don't know what to say either. "I'm . . . uh . . . here with my parents. Visiting someone."

She nods. "Me too." She looks at her mom.

"Well," Leah's mom says. "The care here is excellent." She steps up and shakes my hand. "I'm Leah's aunt Kathleen."

"Oh." She's not Leah's mom. I wonder who they're visiting, but I know enough about not wanting to talk about it to know I shouldn't ask. "I'm Charlie. I've seen you at dance."

She tips her head. "Are you in Leah's class?"

"No. I'm in Advanced Beginner, but I'm hoping I'll do well at the next feis and—" And I stop. Because it seems weird to be talking about Irish dancing here.

"I saw you dance at the nursing home performance this fall," Leah says. "You're really good. You're totally ready for Novice."

"We should head inside," Leah's aunt says. "Are you going back in, Charlie?"

"Yeah, I should." The meeting is probably over by now. Mom and Dad will wonder where I am. Plus Sedgewick is eyeing my scarf again.

"Are you going to the Albany feis?" Leah asks. I nod, and she starts chattering away as if we're walking into dance class or school or someplace normal. "I love that one. They have it at the college, and the gymnasium is huge. They had four different stages last year, and then they do the championship round in the student center."

She pulls open the door, and we step into the lobby. "They even have good food."

"That's like the feis of my dreams," I say. "I've had more five-dollar slices of dried-out pizza than I can count since I started Irish dance."

"I know, right?" She laughs, but then her eyes drift away from me, and her smile turns sad. She waves. And the mom who was sitting beside me at the meeting—*I'm Carolyn, and I'm an addict*—waves back.

Chapter 15

The Sixth Wish

"That's my mom," Leah says, and I don't know what to say back.

I'm-Carolyn-and-I'm-an-addict is someone's *mother*. Leah's mother.

"Oh," I finally manage. It's awful enough having Abby here. Having your mom on drugs must be ten times worse. Moms are supposed to take care of you. They're supposed to—

"Look," Leah says. "I don't know who you're here to see, but . . . if you want to sit with us at brunch . . ." She trails off.

I find my voice. "Sure. I'll talk to my parents. We're visiting my big sister. She's . . ." I think of Leah, of all those people in the meeting, just putting it out there, saying it out loud because it's the truth. "She's addicted to heroin."

"I'm sorry," Leah says. "That's . . . my mom is too. This is the fourth time she's been in here. That's why I live with my aunt now. I used to live in New York."

"You went to a special school for performing arts, right? Catherine told me."

She nods and smiles. "It's a magnet school, so if you love the arts—painting, singing, dancing, whatever—you can go there no matter where you live in New York. I miss it so much." She sighs. "I better go see her."

Mom and Dad and Abby walk up as Leah goes to hug her mom. "Who's that?" Mom asks.

"Her name's Leah. She dances at Miss Brigid's," I say. "Her mom is here."

My mom winces, but then she gets her positive-school-nurse face back. "I'll let her know I can help if Leah ever needs a ride to dance."

I shake my head. "Leah's aunt takes care of her. Besides, she's in Prizewinner. She's really good."

Mom nods. "Well, that's great," she says. But she says it in her chipper school-nurse voice, and I know she doesn't really understand why it matters so much. Mom doesn't *need* that stomping and kicking and forget-everything loudness the way I do, especially now.

I bet Leah needs it even more.

I wasn't looking forward to brunch. I figured it would be rubbery scrambled eggs and cold toast served at cafeteria tables, but the Forest Hills dining room is actually pretty. Someone hung a crystal in every window so the winter sun shoots splashes of rainbow all over the walls. Leah waves us over to a round table where she's sitting with her mom and aunt.

There's a buffet with fresh fruit, ham, bacon, bagels, and eggs. I fill my plate and sit down at the table, where we talk about March weather and the chickens and Irish dance and everything except why we're here. When I go back for more eggs, Jason the movie-star-goat-wrangler-counselor-addict is pouring orange juice.

"Ah, another Forest Hills guest has fallen under the spell of the girls' eggs," he says.

"What girls?"

"Gerta, Red, Izzy, and Octavia," he says, pointing out the window to the hens outside the barn. "Haven't you met them yet?"

"Oh! The chickens!" I feel stupid now. "I mean, obviously I knew the eggs came from chickens. I just didn't realize I knew the chickens personally."

He laughs, and I can't get over how normal and smart and nice he seems. "Can I ask you a question about that meeting earlier?" I lower my voice in case we're not supposed to talk about that stuff at brunch.

But he says, "That's what family visit days are all about. Fire away."

I put the egg spoon back in the buffet pan and look up at him. "When you introduced yourself, you said you were an addict once too?"

"I *am* an addict," he says.

"Still?" My jaw drops. "How can you be a counselor if you're—"

"Here's the thing," he says, cutting me off. "I've been clean and sober six years, but that doesn't mean I'm not an addict. It's not something you get over, like having a cold. Understanding that—having lived through what your sister's living through—makes me a better counselor. I've been there. So it means everything to me to get people through this to a place where they can live again."

I think about that and nod. "I guess that makes sense." There's more I want to ask him—like how people like him and Abby and Leah's mom don't know better than to even try drugs, and why some of the patients are here for the third and fourth time if he's so good at his job—but Mom and Dad are waving me back to the table. "I better go. Thanks," I say.

"Any time. And hey!" he calls as I'm walking away. He pulls a card from his pocket and hands it to me. "You missed the end of our meeting. This is the most important part."

I look down. The laminated card has an ocean scene, and a prayer. "I've seen this before."

"We say it at the end of every meeting, but it's just as important for family members as it is for the addict. It's in the lobby too."

I nod. It's also in Leah's dance bag. "Thanks." I slip the card into my back pocket and sit down to finish my eggs.

We make it home in time for dance class, but I have homework left to do, so I don't stay for the Novice class, and I don't see Leah. I hope she got to stomp good and hard and fast tonight.

Dasha sits beside me, and we unlace our soft shoes. "I can't believe the feis is only three weeks away," she says. "But we are ready, don't you think?"

"Totally. In a way, it's good we missed the other one because we're even more prepared now." Miss Brigid complimented both of us on our slip jig and reel tonight.

I hold up my hand with my fingers spread out. "Five medals. One in each dance, and Novice, here we come. We got this, Dasha."

She high-fives me as Catherine sits down beside us. "What are we celebrating?"

"Nothing yet," Dasha says.

"We're celebrating early, I guess. Feeling good about the Albany feis," I say.

Catherine starts putting on her hard shoes. "You'll do great. I can't wait for that feis. And I'm psyched about science fair now that we're finally getting started."

My good mood fades when I remember they met without me. I told everyone I couldn't go because my parents were making me clean my room. It's a dumb excuse, but it was better than saying I had to go eat eggs with drug addicts. Part of me wants to tell the truth about Abby— tell *somebody* besides Mom and Dad, so the secret doesn't feel so heavy inside me. But part of me still feels ashamed. Like Abby using drugs makes me a bad person somehow. Besides, Dasha has enough problems with the wish-mess I got her into. And Catherine has a flour baby to worry about. Apparently that's not going so well, because I don't see it here with her.

"Where's Meredith?" I ask.

"Shoot!" Catherine grabs her phone, pokes at the keys, waits a second, and then says, "Mom? I have an emergency . . . Can you bring Meredith to dance?" She pauses. "I'm not sure. Try the living room." Another pause. "Maybe the kitchen counter? Or the porch?" She waits again. Then her mom says something, and a look of horror comes over Catherine's face. "Oh no! I can't believe I forgot she was up there. Can you, like, scoop up the flour and put it in a Tupperware or something and babysit until I get home?" She bites her lip. "Okay. Okay. Yeah, I know. Do we have duct tape? Okay . . . bye." She puts her phone down and looks at us. "I left Meredith on top of the car, and she fell off when Mom backed out of the driveway."

"Oh no!" I try not to laugh, even though it's a little funny. It *is* just a bag of flour after all. "Is it . . . is she okay?"

"The bag ripped, but not all the flour came out, so Mom's saving what she can. I'll deal with it when I get home." She sighs. "I am never having real kids."

"Real ones are probably easier to remember. They're not as quiet," I say. "So . . . did you guys get much done for science fair today?"

Catherine shakes her head. "Just some research. We started a chart comparing insects with other kinds of protein like cows and chickens. You can come next week, right?"

"Definitely," I say, even though Mom and Dad will probably make me go to Forest Hills again. "We can meet at my house after school this week too."

Catherine shakes her head. "Can't. I have jazz band until four every day. But we should be okay if we keep meeting on Sundays."

"Sounds good," I lie. I don't want to think about it anymore so I put on my sneakers. Then Dasha and I head outside and run through the sleet to our parents' cars.

I jump in beside Mom and shake frozen rain from my hair.

"Nice weather, huh?" Mom says as she turns for home.

"I hope it gets cold again tonight. There aren't many fishing days left."

"You've become quite the fisherman this winter," she says.

"Fisherwoman." I wipe fog from my window. "My dress fund is up to almost six hundred dollars."

"That's great." She stops at a red light and looks over at me. "I really am sorry we couldn't go to Montreal. I know you were upset."

"Yeah. Sometimes I feel like . . ." I hesitate. But something about the rainy-night quiet in the car makes it feel okay to tell Mom stuff I might not say at home. "Like sometimes Abby takes up all your attention. Even before this whole mess, she had her soccer games and college visits and everything."

Mom nods. "Senior year was pretty busy. And now . . ." She sighs. "Well, this is . . ."

"Awful. I know."

"I'm sorry." Mom reaches across the dark seat and puts her hand on mine. "I know it's been terrible for you too. And it wasn't fair that you didn't get to go to your feis."

"It's okay," I say. "Albany is coming up soon. You can go to that one, right?"

"It's on the calendar," Mom says as we pull into the

driveway. "And Abby will be home by then too. She'd love to watch you dance."

I nod, but when I think about Abby now, I see her at the treatment center. It's hard to picture the old Abby, the one I'd want at the feis with me.

I have a quick turkey sandwich for dinner, gather my stuff for school tomorrow, and get into my pajamas. But before I get in bed, I dig my jeans out of the clothes hamper, pull Jason's card from my pocket, and read it again.

Give me serenity to accept what I cannot change.

When Drew's nana said the prayer, I was thinking about it in terms of small stuff, like missing my feis. That didn't seem small at the time, but it's practically nothing compared to what's happened with Abby. Maybe the prayer is even more important with bigger, scarier things.

I think maybe what it's saying is that what's done is done. I can't go back in time and make Abby keep her D.A.R.E. promise.

Hi, my name is Abby, and I'm an addict.

I missed her saying that when I ran out of the meeting, but I heard Mom and Dad talking on the way home, about how accepting the truth was the first of the twelve steps Abby was going to go through with AA. You have to think about the people you hurt along the way too, and try to make amends.

I wonder if Abby will think about lying to me and hurting Mom and Dad when she gets to that step. I hope so. Maybe that's mean, but I do.

The truth is, I don't feel serene about any of this. But I look down at the card again.

Courage to change the things I can change; and wisdom to know the difference.

I'm not sure this prayer was meant for kids. I can't think of a single thing I can change about this situation. I guess I can change my own stuff. I can keep working toward my dress. I can cheer for Drew when he's being the lake monster at basketball games, and I can help Dasha with her classes. But that doesn't do anything to fix the biggest problem of all.

I put the card in my desk drawer and get ready for bed.

I can't stop thinking about the fish.

I haven't been wishing or even trying to wish since Drew's and Dasha's wishes went kind of wrong. But this is different.

I didn't understand what was happening to Abby this winter. I didn't tell Mom and Dad about the bruises on her arm or the waxed paper bag that wasn't from the donut bakery.

I didn't know.

But now I do. Maybe, if I wish one more wish—a careful one—I can do something to help. Could it really do much harm?

The wishes haven't been perfect, but they haven't been total disasters either. Mom loves her new job. Drew's doing okay even though he has to be the lake monster mascot. I think he's starting to look forward to the first game. Dasha's learning English faster than ever, now that she's in regular classes and we do homework together. So her wish wasn't a total mess.

Even Bobby O'Sullivan's not so bad. He's been too busy helping me tutor Dasha in English and Social Studies to draw note-dragons and write love apps.

Maybe one more wish wouldn't be so dangerous.

And one more wish is all I need.

I fall asleep thinking about how to say it. I scribble ideas in my notebook every time I have a free minute in class on Monday and while I'm working on English with Dasha at lunch. I whisper the words to myself while I'm walking out to the lake with Drew and Mrs. McNeill after school.

The frozen surface is covered in slush now, and our boots leave a trail of dark puddles. Water splashes all over when we drill our holes in the ice, and I wonder how many fishing days we have left. It doesn't matter. I only need to catch the fish one more time.

I drop my line in the water, and when the tug comes, I'm ready. No mumbling or casually worded wishes this time. I'm getting this one right.

I wait for the raspy voice—*Release me, and I will grant your wish*—and I say it:

Let Mom and Dad's health insurance pay for Abby's full month of treatment at Forest Hills, and let her be healthy when she comes home.

I toss the fish back. It flicks its tail in the March sunlight and glimmers before it disappears.

Chapter 16

The Lake Monster Disco

The next day, Dasha, Catherine, and I stay after school so we can cheer for Drew at his basketball game. Catherine sits down on the bleachers and makes room for her flour baby beside her. It's kind of grungy and has a duct tape diaper holding it together since it fell off Catherine's mom's car.

"How's Meredith hanging in there?" I ask.

"She's lost some weight, but I think I'll still pass," Catherine says. "She's tougher with the duct tape. She looks kind of rugged with her scars, don't you think? Like a biker baby."

I laugh, then look around the bleachers to see who else is here. I know Drew's parents are working—I'm not sure how excited his dad would be about this anyway—but Mrs. McNeill is here with a big sign she made. There's a lake monster with "Go, Lakeside Champs!" in a speech bubble.

"Doing my part to support the team," she calls when she sees me. "And its reluctant mascot too."

"Charlie! Charlie!" I recognize Bobby's voice booming across the gym even before I see him, standing on his orange-sneaker tiptoes, searching the crowd.

Dasha waves to him, and his whole face lights up.

"Aw, did you have to do that?" I say. "I was hoping for one Bobby-free afternoon."

"He is not so bad," Dasha says. "In coding club, he's funny and helps people a lot. He only acts strange around you."

When she says that, I have a flash of sympathy for Bobby. Things were probably better for him before I wish-fished him in love with me. So I wave too.

Bobby practically skips up the bleachers. Thankfully, Dasha and Catherine are on either side of me, so he sits by Dasha.

"I didn't know you liked basketball!" Bobby says, leaning across Dasha to talk to me. "Do you come to all the games? Because I can always come to the games, and we can sit together!"

"I came to cheer for Drew," I tell him. "He's the lake monster mascot."

Bobby nods seriously. "I'll cheer for him too. Any friend of yours is a friend of mine."

We don't actually see Drew until the first half is over and he leads the cheerleaders out of the locker room for the halftime performance. His costume is so big it looks like he got swallowed by a giant stuffed animal. His skinny legs are sticking out the bottom with the green tights he hates, and he has huge lake monster flippers on over his shoes, so he has to walk funny or he'll step on his big, webbed toes.

Drew leads the cheerleaders to the center of the court and then turns to face the crowd in the bleachers. "Gimme a C!" he says, without much enthusiasm.

"C!" We all shout back. Bobby is even louder than I am. That guy is dedicated.

"Gimme an H!" Drew calls.

"H!" we holler.

We spell out CHAMPS, and then the cheerleaders do a routine with jumps and cartwheels and a whole lot of whooping. While they're tumbling, Drew is off to the side, dancing a little and giving little kids high fives. He actually looks like he's having some fun.

Then the music starts, and the cheerleaders start a dance routine they've been practicing. Drew looks like he doesn't know what to do, but then he starts dancing too.

"Well, look at that," his nana whispers.

"He's good!" Catherine says.

He is. He tries to do the dance the cheerleaders are doing for a while, but then he breaks into his own routine, which looks like a mix of the electric slide, some pointy-arm disco moves, and swimming. No one's paying any attention to the cheerleaders anymore because Drew is so funny. The more people laugh and cheer, the more he hams

it up. When he starts moonwalking on his giant lake monster feet, everybody gives him a standing ovation.

"Great job, Charlie's friend!" Bobby hollers over the
crowd, and grins at me.

The cheerleaders head for the sidelines, but Drew-
Champ stays out on the court, even after the basketball
players start to come back out. One of the players passes a
ball to another player. Drew-Champ intercepts it, dribbling
with his big green paw toward the basket.

He keeps catching the ball and traveling—I think that's
what it's called when you move without dribbling, which
is illegal—but nobody cares or realizes that Drew plays
this way even when he's not wearing a big fluffy costume.
They think it's part of the act, and it's so, so funny.

Finally, Drew-Champ shoots and misses and throws a
little monster-tantrum out on the court. A ref comes up to
him—probably hoping to finally get the second half of the
game started again—and Drew-Champ pantomimes a big
huge argument with the ref.

"Oh dear." Mrs. McNeill is laughing so hard she can
barely talk, but she manages to say, "I hope he doesn't get
himself in too much trouble."

The ref is laughing, but you can also tell he really wants
the game to start again and doesn't know how to make that
happen. What do you do when a great big monster in skinny
green tights won't get off your basketball court?

You call for help, I guess. The ref waves at the

sidelines, and two more refs start to head out with the coaches. I have a moment of uh-oh panic in my stomach, but Drew-Champ apparently sees them coming and must know the party's over. He throws his green arms up in the air one more time, leaves the first ref, runs to center court, waves at the audience with both paws—we're all cheering like crazy, waving back at him—and runs out the door.

Then they go back to playing basketball.

"Well," Mrs. McNeill says. "That sure was something."

Dasha, Catherine, and I are still laughing when the game ends and we head out to the hallway. Bobby follows us like a stray puppy until his little brother finds him and tugs on his sleeve. "Come on! Mom's waiting outside."

Bobby looks at me. "Can I call you later?"

"Not tonight, okay?" I say. "I've got a ton of homework." I can't help thinking about how long high school is going to be if this wish doesn't wear off. What's this guy going to do when prom rolls around?

"There's Drew!" Catherine points down the hall. He's back in his regular clothes.

"Nice job, Champ," I say when we catch up to him.

He grins. "Thanks. It was more fun than I thought it was gonna be."

"I'd give a million dollars to have that on video," I say.

Drew's whole face drops. "Aw, crud. I never thought of that. Do you think—"

"I think that you were spectacular," his nana says. "And you should enjoy the moment. Your fans are waiting." She points down the hall, where a group of seventh graders are lined up, chanting, "Champ! Champ! Champ! Wooooo!"

While Drew leaves to sign autographs—seriously, they all want his autograph—Dasha, Catherine, and I head for the door. We're halfway through the lobby when Catherine realizes she left Meredith back on the bleachers, so she goes running back to find her.

Dasha and I wait by the sports all-star display and practice some of our dance steps. At one point, we turn so we're dancing toward the trophies. I look into the glass case, and all of a sudden, I can't breathe.

I stop dancing.

Abby is staring out at me from her team photo behind the soccer state championship trophy. Seeing her there, so healthy and strong and happy, makes me feel like someone punched me. I forgot for a little while today. I really did. But now the awfulness is back. This weekend, we'll go to Forest Hills to see the other Abby. The drug addict. Hopefully, my wish will work, and she'll get the full treatment she needs to be better. But I'm starting wonder if life will ever feel the same again.

Chapter 17

Gratitude and Boogers

Mom's on the phone when I get home from Drew's game. She points to the Crock-Pot, so I get myself some soup and sit down at the table. Denver curls up on the floor and flops his head on my foot. He hates soup nights. Nobody drops soup on the floor like they do french fries.

My phone buzzes with a text, and when I look down, I see it's a short one:

Catherine: Uh-oh.

Then there's a link to an online video-sharing site. When I click it, there's Drew, dancing across the gym with his lake monster disco moves. He's going to flip when he sees this. I look to see if I can tell who recorded and shared it because maybe we can get the person to take it down before anybody else sees it. But then I notice it's already gotten two hundred twenty-nine views. In less than an hour.

Uh-oh is right.

"Charlie, do you have a pen?" Mom calls from the counter. I get her one from my backpack, and she writes something while she talks at the person on the phone. "Okay . . . so you need the policy number and then we should be all set?" Mom pauses, listening. "Great. Thank you." She ends the call, puts her phone down, looks up at the ceiling, and whispers it again. "Thank you."

"Who was that?" I ask.

"Insurance company. Dr. Porter was able to convince them to keep Abby in treatment for a full month."

"That was fast," I say. My fish was really on top of this one.

"Fast compared to what?"

"Oh . . . nothing. That's good, isn't it?"

"Very good." Mom pulls a bag of grated cheese from the fridge and holds it up. "Want some mozzarella?"

I nod. She sprinkles it over my soup and says, "Dr. Porter says two weeks isn't long enough to break old habits. Four weeks isn't always either, but that's about the most insurance will cover." She sighs. "I'm so sorry you even have to think about this, Charlie."

"It's okay. I'm happy she's getting better." I'm even happier that this turned out to be one of the things I could change, after all.

The next Sunday, I tell Catherine I can't work on science fair because my parents are making me go to visit my aunt in Vermont. I do have an aunt there, but we don't visit her. We visit Abby at Forest Hills. It's the second weekend of March, but spring still seems a million miles away as we drive through the snow and skate our way across the icy parking lot to the building.

Leah and her aunt aren't around, so I just sit with Mom and Dad and Abby at brunch. When Mom and Dad go with one of the counselors to fill out insurance paperwork, I show Abby Drew's lake monster dancing video, which has gone viral. It has forty thousand views and like two hundred comments, mostly from people saying nice things but a few making fun of his tights. At first, Drew refused to look at the video, but now he loves the attention. He's like a rock star at school. Even the eighth-grade basketball guys cheer when they see him in the hall.

Abby laughs at the video. "That kid has some serious moves," she says. "What about you? How's dance going?"

I show her my new steps on the dining room's hardwood floor. It's not the same without hard shoes, but she claps anyway. "When's your next competition?"

"April second." I hesitate. "You'll be home then, right? Maybe you can come."

"I wouldn't miss it for anything," she says. "Charlie, I owe you an apology."

I stop dancing and look up. Her eyes are teary.

"I know that I did some things that hurt you."

My heart speeds up, even more than it did when I was dancing. "You lied to me. About your arm and that little waxed paper bag in the car. You let me think it was for *donuts*."

She nods slowly. "I lied to a lot of people. Including myself. And I'm sorry." She tugs gently on one of my braids. "I know I can't make it up to you, and I know you probably don't trust me yet. But I'm going to show you that you can. I'm going to be at your feis, I promise."

I look at her and so want to believe in that promise. But having Abby at my feis wasn't part of the wish. And the wish is more important.

"I just want you to get better," I say.

She blinks fast, and a tear slips down her cheek. "Me too."

On the third Sunday in March, Leah and her aunt come to visiting day too. We sit together at the open AA meeting and listen to everyone talk about what happened to them, what scares them now, and what they hope their new lives will look like. We eat brunch and play board games until it's three o'clock and time to leave.

We make it home just in time for dance class. Dasha and I stay to watch the Novice class that I hope we'll be joining soon.

After dance, we all go to Catherine's house to work on our project. When I asked if we could do it later today instead of before class, everybody said sure. Nobody asked why.

But Catherine's known me forever and can tell when something's wrong. While we're in the kitchen getting chips and salsa, she says, "Hey . . . is everything okay?"

"Yeah," I say. "Great. I think the project's going to be fantastic. It's so cool that crickets have more protein per pound than steak, isn't it?"

"It is. But I wasn't talking about the project. You seem . . . I don't know." She crunches on a tortilla chip. "Worried or something. And maybe sad."

When she says that, all my secrets clump together in my throat. They burn my eyes and try to get out, but I shake my head and turn away before Catherine can see. "Nope. I'm okay. I'm really busy because my aunt's been sick, so my parents want us to spend more time with her." I pick up the salsa. "I'll bring this downstairs." And I leave before she can be any nice

For the rest of the night, I sit at the computer, trying to find a place to order mealworms for people food, but all we can find are the ones you feed pet lizards. Drew says it's the same thing, but it just doesn't seem like a good idea to hand out lizard-food samples at a school event.

On the fourth Sunday in March, our car splashes through spring runoff on the roads that lead to Forest Hills. It's been warm this week, and there are mountains all around this place, so the parking lot by the barn is full of giant, cold puddles. Sedgewick is drinking out of one of them when we pull in, but as soon as he sees us, he rushes up to taste Mom's purse.

"I am not going to miss you, goat," she says, pulling the strap out of his mouth.

We go inside, and Abby meets us for the open AA meeting. Jason reads that serenity prayer at the end of every session. Most people close their eyes to listen, but I keep mine open and see Abby mouthing the words silently along with him. I hope she feels like she can change things now.

When we say good-bye to Abby this time, there's no "See you next weekend." Instead, Dad says, "See you Wednesday morning. I'll be here at nine to take you home."

Abby nods and smiles, but her eyes get teary again. Home means our house and not back to school. Abby's not finishing this semester because she missed too much work and her grades were pretty awful to begin with. The plan is for her to live at home for a few months and enroll in the local community college for the summer to try and catch up. Then maybe she can start at another college in the fall.

She's never going back to her old school. The counselors say she can't have contact with any of the friends she used drugs with, so a fresh start would be best. It makes me sad for Abby. UVM was her dream school, ever since she visited the summer before senior year and saw the biology labs where undergrads get to do real research. But if there's one thing I learned listening to all those hi-my-name-is stories from the AA meetings it's that addiction takes a lot of things away from you. Mom says other schools have that kind of research too. She says Abby's lucky she lost her dream school and not her life.

I still think about the fish sometimes. If there were a sure way to wish things right for Abby so she could go back to her old school, I'd do it. But every time I think of how to say it, I imagine a hundred ways the wish could go wrong. I'm leaving this one alone.

I'm really, truly done with wishing this time. A magic fish isn't something you forget right away. But now, every time I start to think about how it could help things, I realize there are better ways.

Last week, Catherine was crying in science because she lost ten more flour-baby points for leaving Meredith on the

floor by her locker. For a second, I caught myself thinking
I'd use the fish to wish Catherine into a better flour-baby
mom. But that wish could get messed up too. And there's
an easier way to help her, anyway. Instead of wishing, I
rummaged through the attic, through my old baby stuff
that Mom could never throw away, and found the Snugli
carrier-thing she used to keep me with her when she was
making dinner.

Now Catherine carries Meredith around strapped to
her chest and hasn't lost a point all week. And I'm finally
starting to think about the fish a little less often.

On Wednesday, Mom gets ready for work, I pack up my
stuff for school, and Dad goes to pick up Abby. It's weird,
but having a normal start to the day makes me so happy
I treble jig down the slush-muddy driveway as I head to
the car. I'm glad we're not all canceling the day like we
did when Abby was admitted. It feels like life can get back
to normal now, like everything isn't an emergency anymore. I never thought I'd feel so grateful for a regular old
Wednesday.

After school, Mom picks me up with the car windows
down. It's gorgeous today—spring cold, but sunny—and
she has her head halfway out the window breathing in
the air.

"You look like Denver." I stick my neck out to the side and pant a little, and she laughs.

"It's nice to see the sun," she says, but I know that's not the whole story. I can tell Mom's as thankful for normal as I am today. "Are you fishing this afternoon?"

"Not today. Drew's nana doesn't like the feel of the ice right now. She says we can't go out until it gets cold again, even though there's still a good ten or twelve inches of ice." Drew's nana worries too much, but I don't care today because I want to get home and see Abby.

There's music blasting from an open kitchen window when Mom and I get out of the car. Katrina and the Waves are belting out "Walking on Sunshine."

Mom laughs. "Sing it, Katrina!"

Dad and Abby are in the kitchen, chopping tomatoes and chili peppers in time to the music. Abby tosses a handful of tomatoes into a bowl, spins around, and sees us. "You're home!"

"*You're* home!" I say, and run to hug her. She smells like the old Abby, like fabric softener and mint gum and her apple shampoo.

And just like that, our family is back to normal.

Dad hands Mom the cheese grater and a block of mild cheddar. "I thought we'd have taco night, then make sundaes and play a little Scrabble later."

"You know it's a school night." Mom looks at me. "Do you have homework?"

"Nope. I did my math in study hall, and we finished an outline for our science fair project at lunch." I grin at Dad and Abby. "Did you guys already pick up ice cream?"

"Ice cream, sprinkles, whipped cream, *and* M&M'S," Abby says.

"Perfect," Mom says. She grates the cheese, and Dad and Abby finish chopping. Dad sautés the meat with taco seasoning, and I put salsa and sour cream in little serving bowls. Denver follows Abby around all night.

"I'm thinking of a word," Abby says.

"Mouth-watering?" Dad guesses.

"That's two words," Abby says.

"Is not. It's hyphenated."

"Doesn't matter anyway. It's wrong. Mom?"

"Gratitude," Mom says, and her eyes get a little shiny. Crying is totally not allowed during the I'm-thinking-of-a-word game, but tonight, it's hard not to be filled with thankfulness.

"I think the word is home," I say.

"You're all wrong," Abby says. "It was booger." She flicks a shred of cheese at Mom. Then we all laugh and eat tacos and ice cream and play Scrabble and laugh some more. It's so good to have Abby home.

Chapter 18

What the Ice Said

It's weird leaving for school Thursday morning and having Abby there at the table, not going anywhere. She can't start at the community college until summer session, and I wonder what she'll do all day until then.

When Mom and I get home after school, I get my answer. Abby's not dancing around the kitchen. She's on the couch crying. Denver is curled up next to her, looking dog-worried. His forehead's all wrinkly.

Mom sends me off to do homework and sits down with Abby to talk. I go to my room and try to do math, but all I can think is that Abby's in trouble again, and my heart pounds so fast I can't even hold my pencil steady. *One day.* We got one day of normal. And what is it now? Please, please don't let her be back on drugs.

I know I shouldn't, but I creep to the stairs and lean

over to listen. At first, all I can hear is Abby sniffling, but then Mom says, "What about reconnecting with some of your high school friends?"

"They're all away at school. Where I'm supposed to be," Abby says, sobbing harder. "And I can't even talk to my best friend."

"No, you can't." Mom's voice is kind but firm. They talked a lot about social groups in the open AA meetings at Forest Hills, how addicts have to cut ties with their old friends who use drugs or it's too hard to avoid using again. I lean against the wall and think about how I'd feel if I couldn't talk to Dasha or Catherine or Drew anymore. Abby must be lonely.

I go downstairs, and Mom looks up from the couch. Abby's still crying, head in her hands, and Mom is rubbing her back. "Charlie, give us a few minutes, okay?"

I shake my head. "I want to help." I sit down on Abby's other side, smushed between her and the arm rest, and wait for her to look up.

When she does, her eyes are wet and red. "I'm sorry. I just . . ." She sighs. "It's like the whole life I had is gone and I'm starting over."

"But that's a good thing. Right?" I reach out and take her hand. Abby used to wear the coolest nail polish ever—skulls and crossbones on Halloween, all sparkly red-and-green for Christmas, or just rainbow polka dots, for no reason at all. Today, her fingernails are ragged and naked. She sees me looking and pulls them back.

"It is good," she says. "I know what I have to do to stay healthy, and I'm doing that. But it's really hard."

"Well, I'm here if you want to hang out. We could go to the mall and get frozen yogurt like we used to. Or play Scrabble or really whatever you want."

Abby's eyes fill with tears all over again. "Thanks." She shakes her head. "Let's do some of that stuff. And I haven't forgotten about your feis either. Did you get your solo dress?"

I look at Mom, and she bites her lip.

"Not yet." I hesitate, but then I say it. "I was supposed to get it the day you ended up at the university health center . . . the day everything happened."

Abby nods slowly. "You were going to get your dress at that other feis. The day I got sick."

"Yeah. But I'm glad you're better now. I can get my dress at the feis in Albany."

Abby takes a deep shaky breath. "I am so sorry. I let everyone down."

Mom doesn't argue with that. Neither do I. It's true. We all know it, probably Abby most of all.

"But you're back now," I say quietly.

"I am. I'm going to stay back." She reaches out with her raggedy nails, takes my hand, and squeezes it. "And

I'm going to cheer for you louder than anybody this weekend."

My solo dress fund is up to five hundred ninety dollars. Six hundred would be great, but when I stop by Drew's house after school, he's not home yet.

"He has a drama club meeting," Mrs. McNeill says.

"When did he join drama club?" Drew didn't say anything about that when we were working on our science project.

"Just happened. They had a last-minute part to fill in the school play. The faculty advisor saw Drew's lake monster video online and recruited him," she says. "So he'll be busy after school all this week. And I'm afraid our fishing season's over anyway, Charlie. Winter magic only lasts so long. All that beautiful sunshine has done a job on our ice."

I look out at the lake. "It's still frozen all the way across. Can't we stay close to shore?"

She shakes her head. "That's honeycomb ice. Nothing but trouble." She looks at me over her glasses. "And don't you even think about fishing on your own."

"I won't."

And I don't. But I do take a walk down to the lake after

dinner. The moon is rising over the ice, and there's a breeze blowing. It was a warm wind up the street, but here, it's picked up the chill of winter. I wrap my arms around myself and step carefully out onto the ice by shore.

I see what Mrs. McNeill means by honeycomb. It's the same frozen water we've been walking on all season, but this is nothing like the clear, dark ice of January. Spring ice is slushy and crunchy, even when it's still plenty thick to walk on.

I walk out a little more. It's okay that we can't fish. I wasn't planning to try and catch the wish fish tonight anyway. I don't need any more wishes now that Abby's better.

I've been thinking for a while about what'll happen when the ice is gone. It's easy to come back to the exact same place to fish when you have a neat round hole marking your spot. Even if we came out near this point in the rowboat this spring, I'd never find the exact same place to drop that line. Even if I did, even if I caught that wish fish, you can't very well make out-loud wishes in a boat full of people.

But none of that matters. My last wish was the one I really needed. Abby got her full month of treatment, and she's home and healthy, even though she's a little sad. She'll figure out stuff to do for a few weeks until school starts. And I'll be there for her. I'll be a better friend than any of those college people were.

I start toward shore, but a sound stops me. A musical, otherworldly twang that's familiar and alien all at once.

I take another step, and the ice sings again. A low, growling thump, followed by a fizzle like you hear when you pour a glass of ginger ale.

The wind blows, and the cedar trees on shore creak, leaning over to listen too. The moon sparkles down on the honeycomb ice, and I stand and stare and breathe it all in. The booming, thumping, gurgling, twanging, chirping, magical ice song. There are no ice flowers tonight, but it's magic all the same.

That ice is talking to me, like it knows what a rough couple of months it's been. Like it knows that the feis is tomorrow.

I hold my breath and listen again.

This is your time, it says.

Shine.

Chapter 19

Dancing as Fast as I Can

When I come downstairs Saturday morning, Abby's at the table, dressed, ready to go, and eating cereal. Mom's rushing around the kitchen packing our snacks.

"Where's Dad?" I ask. "We have to leave in twenty minutes or we won't have time to get my dress."

"Dad's had a rough night," Mom says. "He either has food poisoning or a twenty-four-hour bug. He's a little better now, but he needs to stay home today and get some rest."

Abby looks up from her cereal. "Do you want me to stay back in case he needs anything?"

"No!" I blurt out, and then realize how selfish and little-kid-like that sounds. "I mean, it's just that we'd talked about you coming to see me dance. But that's okay." I look at Mom. "Dad should have somebody to get him Gatorade and stuff."

"Or you can stay with him," Abby says, "and I'll take Charlie. I've been to Albany plenty of times. That college is where we used to do Model UN."

Mom frowns, and I know what she's thinking. She's already let me down with one feis; she needs to be at this one.

"It's totally fine if Abby takes me," I say. And I mean it. I haven't had any real sister-time with Abby in forever, not since before she left for college. "And Dasha's mom is going, so she'll be there, just in case."

Mom looks at me. "Are you sure?"

"Positive."

Fifteen minutes later, Abby and I are driving down Interstate 87 with the windows down and the radio blasting.

"You sure you have everything?" Abby shouts over the music. "Need to make a last-minute run for sock glue?"

"Nope. All set."

She turns down the radio a little. "Do you ever stop in the middle of a jig and think to yourself, 'How is it that I ended up in a sport where gluing my socks to my legs is a requirement?'" She loves teasing me about the weird stuff that goes along with Irish dancing. The wigs and spray tans that the older girls wear are even crazier, if you ask me.

"Sock glue's not that bad," I say. "It's better than the butt glue gymnasts use to keep their leotards from creeping up."

"Butt glue!" Abby shouts and laughs. And I laugh too. Not because butt glue is that funny but because Abby is Abby again. I missed her so, so much.

We get to the feis in plenty of time, unload the car, and head inside.

"This is perfect," I say. "We're nice and early to get a good camp site."

"And here I am without my marshmallow stick," Abby jokes. But with the exception of the bonfires, hanging out at a feis really is a lot like camping. There are stages for the dancing and tables for the judges, and other than that, everybody sets up their own little areas, with blankets and the kind of folding chairs people take to soccer games and picnics. Abby and I brought two chairs, a blanket, and the cooler Mom filled with our water and snacks.

We pass booths full of feis vendors' stuff. There's a table full of sparkly socks and another one with ribbons and crowns. The wig lady is set up in a corner, helping a tiny girl pull on a curly red wig twice the size of her head.

"Oh! There's Catherine!" I jump up and down and wave until she sees me from the booth where she's shopping. She waves back and turns to pay for her sequined socks.

Abby squints at Catherine. "What's she got in that weird pouch?"

I laugh. Catherine has the Snugli carrier strapped over her solo dress. "That's Meredith. Her flour baby."

"Ohh . . ." Abby nods. "I remember that project. I hope it doesn't leak on her dress."

Abby and I choose a strategic camping spot, not too close to the bathrooms and within sight of the main stage and results wall. When you dance at a feis, you don't find out how you did right away. After the judges send in their papers, the results get posted on the wall, so it's good to have a camp site where you can see when things are happening over there.

"Ready to go shopping?" Abby bounces on her sneakers. She might mock my sock glue, but she loves looking at solo dresses. Some of them are so fancy, full of sequins and crystals and everything. I can't believe I'm finally getting one.

"The dress room is over there by where we came in." I take my wallet from my dance bag—it's all fat and heavy with fishing money—and we head that way.

"Do you know what you want to get?" Abby asks.

"Maybe something blue. Mom says that would look good with my eyes. But I need to see what they have. Definitely used. New ones cost too much. There's a designer named Gavin Doherty whose dresses are supposed to be the best. They're like two or three thousand dollars."

"Dude, that's more than my car!"

"I know, right? And they're so famous that people just use the designer's first name to describe the dress. They'll say, 'Oh, is that a Gavin you're wearing?' And then I always picture the person dancing with a little Irish guy draped over her shoulders."

Abby laughs and then draws in her breath as we step into the dress room. Everything is so bright and sparkly it's like walking into a Rainbow Fish book. The dresses are all displayed on racks. Kids and moms are pawing through them, holding them up. There's lots of "How about this one?" and big eyes and head shakes and "No, too much. But maybe this?"

Abby picks up a black dress with pink swirls and crystals. "Do you like this one?"

"Not really. Too much pink." I'm not big on pink. "Plus, look at the tag."

Abby takes a look at the fifteen-hundred-dollar price tag and pretends to have a coughing fit. She puts the dress back and picks up a white one with twisty red designs. "This looks like the structure of DNA." For a second, she looks sad that she's not back in Vermont learning about it. But then she grabs another dress—an orange one with lots of silver sequins.

"Oh, that one's nice!" I duck into the makeshift dressing room and try it on over my shorts and tank top. "Nope. Too small."

By the time I'm out of the dress, Abby has three more for me to try. Only one fits, and it's six hundred fifty dollars. "Over my budget." I pass it back to Abby to hang up.

Then a girl comes out of the dressing room next to me with a white dress that's the most gorgeous thing I've ever seen. It has ribbons of yellow and purple and green down the front, all woven with silver sequins and tiny crystals. It's perfect. The girl holds the dress out to her mom, and I hold my breath.

"What did you think?" the mom says.

"It was too tight on top," the girl answers, and starts to put it back. I make big eyes at Abby and point wildly, and Abby has that dress in her hand before the hanger touches the rack. She helps me put it on. I want to see it so badly I can hardly hold still while she zips the back.

"Does it feel okay on top?" Abby asks.

I raise my arms and wiggle around a little. "It's fine." I step in front of the mirror and suck in my breath. It's so pretty it doesn't even look like me.

"That's gorgeous," Abby says. "You have to get it."

I hold my breath and reach for the tag. I didn't want to look before I knew if this was the dress or not. Now that it is, now that I want it so much, I'm wishing I had that fish back in my hand so I could wish for this tag to say the right thing.

I flip it over. "Yes!" I wave the tag at Abby. "It's only five hundred!"

Abby motions me to turn. "Let's get you unzipped. If you want to go get ready, I'll stay and pay for this while you use the bathroom and stuff."

I look at the clock and realize I'm dancing in half an hour. "Oh, wow—thanks!" I hand Abby my wallet and give her a super-quick hug. Then I take one last look at my beautiful, amazing dress and run to get ready.

Dasha's in the ladies' room when I get there. Her mom's braiding her hair in the mirror, so I give her a quick hug from the side and start brushing mine at the next sink over.

"Did you find a dress?" she asks.

"I did. It's white with colors kind of winding through it. My sister's paying for it now, so I'll show you when we line up to dance."

"I can't wait!" Dasha says. She's in her school uniform—a white blouse and blue jumper with green embroidery—but the shiny green ribbons Dasha's mom has braided into her hair makes it look fancier than usual. She grins at me in the mirror. "Five dances, five medals today, right?"

"Right!" I finish in the bathroom and hurry back to our campsite. Abby has my dress laid out over my dance bag. She holds up my wallet. "Where do you want this? You've got like ninety dollars left in here."

"In my bag is fine," I say. "The stage is right there, so we'll never be out of sight of it."

Abby helps me put my new dress on over my shorts and tank top, and then I put on my soft shoes.

"What's first?" Abby asks.

"Slip jig, and the reel is pretty soon after that. I'll be fine with those, but I'm a little worried about my treble jig because—"

"Hey!" Abby's face lights up. She looks past me, waving. When I turn, there's a girl about Abby's age walking toward the stage with a smaller girl in a solo dress.

"Will you be around a while?" the girl calls.

Abby nods and turns back to me. "Sorry, that's my friend Olivia. I had no idea she was going to be here."

"Is that her little sister?" I ask.

"Must be." Abby shrugs. "Sorry . . . tell me about your dance."

"I should actually go get ready." Dancers are lining up near our stage, so I hurry over and squeeze in next to Dasha. Irish dancers usually go two at a time during competitions, but we won't be at the same time. You never really get to dance with someone from your own school. "Good luck," I whisper.

"You too."

Chapter 20

Waiting and Wondering

Once the judges have their pens and clipboards ready, a feis volunteer nods, and two girls in super-fancy solo dresses step up to go first. The accordion player beside the stage starts to play, and the girls bounce into motion. They're okay but not great. Miss Brigid would be all over them for not keeping their toes out.

Dasha and a shorter girl in a blue solo dress go next. Dasha's great. She has this tight discipline about her dancing that nobody else in our class can really match. Her moves look so perfect and exact. She looks twice as good next to the other girl, who isn't even pointing her toes at the right times.

I give Dasha an excited smile when she comes off the stage. Two more girls dance, and then it's my turn. I try not to pay any attention to the other girl on stage with me, but

I can't miss seeing the zillion crystals on her dress. Then I look down at my own dress—my amazing, color-braided, sparkling dress that I worked for myself—and I just want to dance.

So I do. My slip jig isn't perfect, but it's pretty close, and when it's all over, I rush up to Dasha and hug her and squeal. "We did it! Don't you think? You were so good! We have to be top three."

She smiles. "We won't know for a little while, I guess." She looks over at her mom, who's tapping her watch. "We have the reel in fifteen minutes. Do you want to come with my mom and me to get some water?"

"Sure, let me see if my sister wants to come."

I find Abby near the judges' table, talking with her friend Olivia. "I'm going to get something to drink with Dasha," I say. "Want to come?"

"No, I'm okay." Abby turns to her friend. "Liv, this is my sister, Charlie."

"Nice to meet you." I shake her hand and hope mine aren't too sweaty.

"Abby says you know that dancing lake monster guy from YouTube. That's so cool!"

"You saw that?"

"Everybody's seen it at school. Our sorority had a lake monster dance party with green cupcakes and stuff, and we had it up on a big screen. That kid's awesome."

"He's pretty cool," I say. Then I turn to Abby. "Sure you don't want anything?"

"No thanks. Do you need money?" Abby asks.

"I have some. Thanks!" I grab my wallet and cell phone from my bag and find Dasha and her mom at the snack bar. We get bottled water and split a bag of corn chips. I lean way, way forward so no crumbs get on my new dress.

Just as we're finishing, my phone dings with a text.

Hi, Charlie! Bobby here! (But I bet you knew that—LOL.)
Good luck at your feis today! <3 <3 <3

I look at Dasha. "How'd Bobby know about the feis?"

She laughs. "I might have mentioned it at coding club this week. He texted me too. I thought it was nice."

She shows me her text from Bobby, which is the same except it has a smiley face instead of less-than-three hearts. "He even spelled feis correctly," she says.

I have to admit, that's impressive. But I still hope this wish wears off.

Dasha looks at the clock on the snack bar wall. "We'd better go get ready."

Dasha goes to find her mom, and I head for our home base to put my wallet and phone away. Abby and her friend are camped out on the blanket laughing and talking when I get back. It's good to see her happy again.

"Time for the next one?" Abby stands and stretches her legs while I put my wallet away in my dance bag.

"Yep. The reel and the light jig. Then we change into hard shoes for the rest of the day."

"Lead the way."

The reel and light jig go even better for both Dasha and me, and by the time we're done, my eyes are glued to the results wall. "I wish they'd hurry up. I mean—ohmygosh look!"

One of the feis volunteer moms is walking to the wall with her hands full of papers and tape. We race over, wait for her to finish taping, and find our levels and age groups. Dasha and I scream at the same time. She got first place in the slip jig, and I got second. We hang around the wall until the reel and light jig results come in, and then we scream and hug all over again. In both of those, I'm one, and she's two.

I look for Abby to tell her. She's over watching Olivia's little sister on the Beginner stage. I can't wait for the music to end, so I hurry up behind her and tug on her curly pony-tail. "Dasha and I got first and second," I whisper, and Abby gives me a huge hug.

We have pizza for lunch—very careful pizza so I don't end up with sauce splotches on my amazing best-dress-ever—and then Dasha and I change into hard shoes and line up for our treble jig. Our last two dances are back to back, so there's no time to check results in between.

"You got this, Charlie," Abby tells me right before I start my treble jig. When I finish and look up, she's the first person I see, standing behind the judges' table, clapping like crazy.

"How long before the next one?" she asks after I get off the stage.

"Fifteen minutes." I'm still catching my breath from the jig.

"I'll be right back, okay? I'm going to run out and get something to eat with Liv."

"I think the café's still open. The pizza's not bad."

"Yeah . . . I think we're going to get wings," she says, and glances toward the door to the parking lot. "There's a place down the street. I'll be back for your dance."

"Okay." I leave to find Dasha, and we watch dancing on the other stages until it's time to line up for the hornpipe, our last dance of the day. I don't see Abby yet, but I'm not near the beginning of this lineup, and I know she'll be back soon.

Dasha goes first. She's incredible, like always. She doesn't even look tired, which is great because one of the things we get judged on is endurance.

I'm in the last group. I step onto the stage and hear my hard shoes click across the wood as I take my spot. I look out over the huge room of dresses and crazy wigs and swirling accordion notes, and even though my legs are tired and I'm sweating in my new dress, I feel so full of music that I can't wait to start.

I know Abby's back by now, but there's no time to look for her in the crowd. The judge nods. The accordion player starts playing. I spring into motion, arms at my sides and feet flying.

This song is the fastest. This dance is the hardest. And even though it should be tiring me out, the music fills me up more and more, with every click and every kick.

I stomp and jump, and the noise echoes off the plywood stage floor, all over the huge room. Other stomps from other stages answer back. This day, dancing in my shining dress with my sister here watching, is more full of magic than any wish fish in any fairy tale. When the music ends, I stand with my toes out, my arms up, out of breath and full of anticipation.

Dasha is waiting for me at the edge of the stage. "That was so great!" she says. "I want results nowwwwww!" She pretends to faint. I laugh and look for Abby, but I still don't see her. I really hope she got back in time because that last dance might be the best I'll ever do at a feis. Everything about it felt perfect.

"Do you want to get something to—oh, look!" Dasha points to the volunteer table near the results wall. One of the feis ladies is standing up with a handful of paper and tape. "Could that be ours already?" Her eyes are huge.

"Maybe. Should we check?" Part of me wants to fly across the room and tackle that lady with the papers, but another part of me wants to wait. Because once we get our results, there'll be the awards ceremony with the medals and cheering, and then this day—this incredible, perfect day—will be over.

I wish it could last forever.

But I also really want to see those results.

"Let's go!" I race Dasha across the room. I almost wipe out because I slip on my hard shoes—I need to put more tape on the bottoms—and skid into the results wall.

"Well, someone's excited," the feis lady says, grinning with her pile of papers. "Which group and age level are you?"

"Advanced Beginner," I say. "Under fourteen."

Dasha and I lean in while she rifles through her paper stack. She looks up at me. "You both need to take like three steps back. I don't want to get knocked over when I put these up." She holds a few papers high over her head, so we can't see what's on them.

"Sorry!" We jump back and bounce on our toes. The woman puts the papers up, steps back, and holds up her arm to invite us in. "There you go, girls."

Dasha and I fly to the wall like paper clips to a magnet, and I try to take in the information all at once.

I have a third in the treble jig and first in the hornpipe.

Dasha has a first and a second.

"We did it!" I hug her. "We placed in all five. Five medals!" I step back and hold up my hand, with my five fingers stretched out.

Dasha smiles and says, "Now we move up to Novice!"

Her mom rushes up and hugs her. "I just saw. Oh, girls, congratulations! You did so well today!"

I turn to look for Abby, but she's not around the wall. "I need to go back to our stuff and find my sister," I say. "You're staying for awards, right?"

Dasha shakes her head. "Mama needs to get back. Can you bring my medals home?"

"Sure!" I say. "Although ten medals between the two of us might be heavy."

She laughs. "You're a big, strong Novice girl now. You can handle it."

I wave and head back to our campsite, and now I'm finally feeling a little tired. In the best way ever, though. Like I danced out every bit of this crummy winter and now only good things are ahead.

Abby's not back yet, or maybe she's gone to the bathroom. I have to go too, so I head for the ladies' room. I find a mom to unzip my dress—you can do that with Irish dance moms; they all take care of all the kids. Then I change into yoga pants and my favorite T-shirt. I got it at a feis last year. It's bright green with white lettering that says: Irish Dancers Kick Butt.

The whole time I change my clothes, I listen for Abby's voice. She should have been back for my dance, and even if she didn't make it, she should be here by now. I zip my dress into its carry bag and tell myself that she'll be sprawled out on our blanket when I get there. She probably got back in time to see me dance. And then after that, she was probably in a different bathroom or in the café getting me water or a soda, and when I get back to our camp, she'll be there. She will. She'll be waiting to hug me and tell me what an amazing job I did.

I walk through the crowded room, telling myself all those things.

But when I get back to our blanket, Abby's not there.

And now my heart is racing because I know something's wrong. What if she and her friend got in a car accident? Or got food poisoning like Dad or something else awful happened?

No.

No. Maybe they got stuck in traffic. This isn't home, where the only traffic is five cars at a red light. This is Albany, and it's a city, and there are way more cars and way more people, so they're late. That's all.

I take a deep breath. I'm going to get myself a soda at the café now. Maybe Abby will be there, but even if she's not, that's fine because she'll be back soon.

I unzip my dance bag to get my wallet.

And that's gone too.

Chapter 21

Last Ice

There was this guy at the treatment center—Brent or Trent or something—who talked about his heroin addiction at one of the open AA meetings.

"I was so desperate I stole money from my mother," he said. "My own mother." He shook his head, and somebody said something positive to him about how far he's come since then, but all I remember thinking was that he was a totally awful person. What kind of person does that?

Now I know.

The kind of person who doesn't care about her family. The kind who lies to them. The kind who comes home from treatment all full of healthy food and promises, takes her little sister to a dance competition, and then bolts.

I find my cell phone in my bag—at least Abby didn't run off with that too—and call her. It rings and rings and goes to her voice mail. "Hey, it's Abby! You know what to do!"

I want to throw the phone across the room because no, I don't know what to do. The person who brought me here took off, and I have no idea where she is and I don't even have a ride home. But I don't throw the phone. I call Mom and tell her that Abby's gone.

"Gone where?" I hear the panic in her voice.

"I don't know. She took off with her friend a long time ago and—"

"*What* friend?"

"Her name is Olivia. They said they were getting something to eat."

"Well, maybe—"

"And she took my money."

I hear Mom's breath rush out.

"Okay," she says, "I'm going to—Charlie, who else is there from your dance school? Can you get a ride home with someone?"

"Dasha was here with her mom, but they left." I look around the room. Rachael's not here because there was a bigger feis in Ohio this weekend. I don't see Catherine, and I don't want to ask her for a ride anyway because I'd have to tell her why I need one. "I don't think anybody else is around." The words are just out of my mouth when I see Leah come out of the bathroom with her aunt. She's still in her dress—the better you are, the later you dance. And she already knows about Abby, so it would be okay asking. "Leah's here with her aunt. I'll ask if I can go home with them. What about Abby?"

"Dad and I will take care of Abby," Mom says.

So I hang up. I find Leah and her aunt. When I tell them what happened, both of their faces fall. They look so sad for me I can't stand it. I wonder if Leah's mom ever left her somewhere without a way to get home.

Leah finishes her last dance. I stand with her aunt Kathleen and watch, and we clap when she's done. I keep looking around for Abby, hoping she might breeze in with a box of chicken wings and a funny story about how they had to wait forever for it.

I wish as hard as I can. But my fish is miles and miles away.

Abby doesn't come. She doesn't come for the last dance. She doesn't come for the awards ceremony, so only Leah and her aunt are there to see me pick up my five medals for placing in all five dances I needed to move up to Novice. I pick up Dasha's too, and they all clink together.

I'm finally clinking. That should make me happy.

It doesn't.

Abby doesn't come to help clean up our stuff, so I have

to pack our chairs and fold the blanket and carry everything out to Leah's aunt's car.

I look for Abby once more, in the parking lot.

She's not there either.

When Leah and her aunt drop me off at home, Mom's car is in the driveway.

"I'll see you at dance tomorrow," Leah says. "I hope everything's okay," she adds, even though we all know it's not.

Her aunt squeezes my hand. "I'll say a prayer. Call me when you learn something, okay?"

I nod and say thanks, but what is it she thinks we're going to learn? Where Abby is? I know where she is . . . off with her friend and my money doing drugs somewhere, even though she's supposed to be all better now.

I step into the kitchen, and Mom's on the phone. She's not saying much, just listening and blinking a lot.

"Okay." She scratches something down on a notepad. Then she takes a shuddery breath. "Call when you know anything. Love you too," she says. On the last word, her voice breaks, and she sinks to the floor.

"Mom?"

She's leaning against the cabinets under the sink, hugging her phone to her chest, crying and shaking. Denver's standing next to her whining. Even he knows something awful is wrong. "Mom! What's going on? Where's Abby?"

Mom doesn't say anything. She just keeps crying and holds up her arms. I don't know if I'm supposed to sit down and hug her or help her get up, and I'm terrified because my mother—my school-nurse-everything-is-under-control mother—is out of control on the kitchen floor, and no one is here to help.

"Mom, it's going to be okay." I drop my dance bag and sit down next to her, and she pulls me into a tight hug. Her body is heaving with sobs. I don't know what to do except hold on.

Finally, Mom catches her breath and pulls away from me. "Abby . . ." She chokes on a sob and squeezes her eyes closed for a few seconds. Then she takes a long, shaky breath and says, "Abby overdosed on heroin this afternoon, Charlie. They've got her at Albany Medical Center. Dad's there now."

"No." I shake my head. Abby was fine. She was singing in the car with me on the way to the feis. She was clapping for me after my slip jig and laughing with her friend, and yeah, maybe they ditched me, but how can she all of a sudden be in the hospital?

I can't catch my breath, but finally I manage to ask, "Is she going to be okay?"

Mom presses her lips together tightly, like she's trapping words inside. She squeezes her eyes shut, then finally opens them and looks at me. "I don't know." She takes a shaky breath and grabs my hand so tight it hurts. "They gave her a drug to try and reverse the overdose, but . . ."

She doesn't finish her sentence, and she doesn't need to because I know. I know from all those awful stories at the awful open AA meetings. I've heard that sentence finished a hundred times.

. . . but it doesn't always work.

. . . but an overdose can be fatal.

. . . but my sister might die.

"She can't die. Abby can't die," I say, and furious tears stream down my face. "How could she *do* this again?"

Mom shakes her head. "She didn't, it's just— She's sick, Charlie."

"But she got *help!*" I shout. It makes Mom wince, and I don't care. "She got help, and that stupid treatment center was supposed to *fix* this!"

Denver stands up and barks once, then shifts his weight between his front paws.

Mom pulls him in close to her and strokes his fur. "Shhh . . ." She looks down and presses her hands into her eyes. When she looks up again, she's not crying any more new tears. But she looks so, so tired and sad. "Help isn't magic." She takes a deep breath and stands up. "I have to go to the hospital, Charlie."

"Okay. Let me get changed." I start to get up, but she puts up her hand.

"No. You need to stay home this time. It's too . . . it's just too much." She looks down at her phone. "I'll call Mrs. McNeill and see if she can come over for a while."

"No." I reach for the phone—too fast—and knock it out of her hand. It bounces off the table and onto the floor. A part falls off, and the battery skids across the linoleum.

Mom curses—she never curses—and I scramble to pick up the phone pieces. "I'm sorry! I wasn't trying to—I'll go next door and talk to Mrs. McNeill while you get ready. Her car's there, and I'm sure she'll come right over. I'm sorry, Mom!"

Mom's shoulders sink. "No, I'm sorry. And yes, please see if she's around." She takes the pieces of her phone from me and turns to go upstairs.

I don't bother to put on my coat. I step outside, and the wind off the lake blows right through my sweatshirt. It's howling in big, loud gusts tonight, and the ice is talking again, but I don't stop to listen.

I turn down the sidewalk to the McNeills' house. The garage door is open with the ice fishing sled inside. It's still loaded up, even though we haven't been out in a week.

I turn back to the lake and listen.

The ice groans and creaks and thunders. I know just how it must feel, wanting to hold on. Knowing there's nothing it can do.

But there's one thing left that I can do tonight.

The fish has never been perfect, but it's always kept its promise. My wish for the health insurance people to pay for Abby's treatment worked. It did. It just wasn't enough.

Abby needed bigger magic. And the fish is still out there.

I can catch it one more time, and this time, I'll wish better.

I *have* to wish better. It has to work.

Please, please, please . . . I think.

I run to the garage and find a fishing rod with a lure on the end. I pull the rod out and knock a tackle box to the floor. It clatters open on the concrete, and lures spill out. The McNeills' porch light goes on, but I can't stop to pick up the lures, and I can't stop to explain. There's no time.

I run across the yard to the rocks, pumping my arms, sliding on the melting ice and snow. The moon lights up a thin border of water right along the shore, but the ice beyond that is plenty thick and safe. I jump over the sliver of open water. When I land, my feet slide out from under me and I fall on my back, but it's okay. The fishing pole doesn't break. I crawl out until the ice is a little less slippery. Then I stand and run.

The ice crunches and sloshes under my sneakers. They're soaked through, but I'm halfway there now. I can see the dark spot on the ice, the hole where the fish is— *Please. One more time.*

I'm shaking from cold and my fingers are numb and my hands are trembling, but I get the line down into the hole, into the water below.

Come on. Come on!

The wind blows, and there's a sound like the sky is ripping open, far away. The ice here on the bay is fine, but out on the broad lake it's breaking up. Giant slabs crash against one another, scratching and clunking, frigid water sloshing over them.

I bounce my line in the water.

Come on!

Finally, there's a tug.

Yes!

I step back to reel it in. Just as that glimmering green eye appears over the lip of the hole, the ice beneath me makes an awful, cracking splash and falls away.

Slush-cold water swallows me up to my neck. It squeezes my body all around.

I fling out my arms. The pole goes flying. I grab at the edge of the ice, but then the edge is gone, and the water is cold, so cold I can't breathe, and I can't see the ice or the pole or the fish.

I wish . . .

I can't wish.

I can't breathe.

I need to get out.

I flail at the edge of the ice. I kick forward and try to pull myself out, but it's wet and cold, so cold, and my arms slip back.

"Help!" I cry and gasp for air.

Not loud enough.

Too much wind. Too little breath.

There's no one to hear, and the fish—where is it? I can't catch my breath.

I think I hear my name, but no one is there, no one can help. I try again to pull myself out. I put my hands flat on the edge and push, but the ice breaks like a potato chip. I reach again. I try to hold on, just hold on, but my shoes are pulling and my legs are heavy, and I'm shaking, and then something hard and scratchy slaps my cheek.

"Grab the rope!"

But there is no rope. I don't see rope, and if I let go of the ice, I'll sink and it's cold.

"Grab the rope!"

The rope hits me, loops around me. I push up on my elbows to reach—and the ice breaks again, but this time, this time, I have the rope in my frozen hands. I can't feel them. I can barely hold on, but I hug the rope as tight as I can and feel a tug.

A tug—yes! Reel it in . . .

I wish . . .

This one is bigger, but I hold on.

I wish . . .

Chapter 22

The Seventh Wish

When I wake up, Mom is there with a nurse.

"It's okay." Mom puts a hand on my cheek. "You're going to be okay. You fell through the ice, but Mrs. McNeill found you. You're safe now."

I nod because I remember. The ice was there and I had the fish and then the ice was gone and it was so cold and every time I tried to get out the edges broke off again. Now I'm here, and I never wished. I never let the fish go. It must be frozen solid out on the ice with my lure still in its mouth. I never got to wish, and now the fish is dead and it's too late.

I start to whisper Abby's name, but my lips don't move. And it's warm.

My wet clothes are gone. There are blankets all around me. It's warm here, and I'm so tired.

I close my eyes again.

Later, someone puts a hand over mine, and I open my eyes again. Mom is there with Mrs. McNeill and a nurse. There's an IV in my arm, and the nurse is doing something with a clear bag hanging on a rack.

"What is that?" I whisper. My throat hurts.

"Just fluids," the nurse says, "to keep you hydrated. Try to rest. You gave your family a scare."

She leaves, and I look at the line that snakes from the bag to my bed, the needle-thing taped to the crook of my arm. And I remember.

"Mom, where's Abby? Is she still—"

"In the hospital in Albany. Dad's with her. The emergency treatment worked. The doctors say she's going to be all right."

"Good," I whisper. But then my eyes fill with tears, and I say, "No . . ." because if Abby were all right, she never would have left me at the feis. That Abby who walked out and took my money was hi-my-name-is-Abby-and-I'm-an-addict and not the old Abby. Not my sister. "She's not all right, Mom." And there's nothing I can do for her, now that the fish is gone.

"Shh . . ." Mom brushes my hair back on my forehead. "I know that, Charlie. Even before this happened, we knew that relapse is often part of an addict's recovery." She takes a deep, shaky breath. "They even warned her that if she injected heroin again, the same amount could kill her because her body wasn't used to it anymore."

"And she did it anyway." I shake my head because I can't understand. I can't. "She knew, Mom. How could she do that? How was she not afraid?"

Mom sucks in her breath. "I don't know. I guess addiction is bigger than fear. Bigger than lots of things." She looks at me. "How were you not afraid of going out on the ice tonight?"

"I don't know." But that's a lie. I haven't been afraid of the ice since the first wish. And not being scared felt awesome and free. Until it didn't.

Anyone should have known that ice was dangerous tonight. Honeycomb ice, Mrs. McNeill called it. She'd warned me a person could fall right through. I *heard* the ice breaking up in the waves. I *heard* those huge chunks smashing together. And I still wasn't scared. "I should have been afraid. But I wanted to help Abby."

"What?" Mom looks at me. What I said doesn't make sense to her. How could it? She doesn't know about the fish, and I can't tell her now. She'll think I have brain damage from falling in that icy water.

I start to cry. I can't believe I did this to Mom when she's already such a mess over Abby.

"Shh . . . I'm sorry. Try to rest." Mom shakes her head. "I know it's hard, but you can't help Abby, Charlie. Neither can I. Abby's the only person who can do that. And now she has another chance. She's lucky."

I shake my head. Lucky is when you win the lottery or a big stuffed animal at the fair. Abby's on a bed in some hospital far away with another broken promise sitting on her chest. Now she'll have to go through treatment all over again, and maybe it will work and maybe it won't, and maybe she'll stay clean and live and maybe she won't and she'll die next time. Abby's not lucky.

"You're lucky too," Mrs. McNeill says, stepping up to my bed. I've never seen her cry, but her eyes are teary. "I'd have never taken you out fishing if I thought you'd go running off on your own."

"I'm sorry," I whisper. I want to tell her why I did it. I want to tell her about the fish, but I can't. The best I can do is, "Somehow, I got it in my head that the ice was magic . . . and I thought . . . I was going to make a wish. A wish for Abby, that . . ." I stop because it doesn't make any sense at all.

But Mrs. McNeill nods slowly. "You know the thing about magic, Charlie? We can wish on clovers and shooting stars and ice flowers all we want. But in the end, the only real magic is what's inside us and the people we love. Some things are beyond even that magic." She reaches inside her collar and pulls out the four-leaf clover charm. "It took me a long time to learn that."

I nod. Even if she can't know about the fish, somehow Mrs. McNeill understands. Knowing that helps a little, but it also makes me feel worse about what I did. I wonder if she knows about her fishing pole. "Mrs. McNeill, I have to tell you something else. I took your fishing pole from your garage tonight."

I don't use the word "stole," even though that's what I did. I stole a fishing pole from Drew's nana, who trusted me and took me out fishing almost every day this winter. What kind of person does that? A desperate one. One who can only think of one thing.

"I'm sorry," I say again. "It might still be out there." I don't tell her there might be a dead magic fish on it.

"And there it will stay," she says. "I'm not worried about the pole. I was worried about you. I'm glad you're all right, but if you ever want to fish with me again, you have to promise you'll never set foot on that ice without a buddy."

"I promise," I say. And I mean it. My fear of the ice is back. Maybe it's because the fish died and that reversed the wish. Or maybe it's because I almost died. It doesn't matter. I can't imagine going out there again.

Mrs. McNeill heads home, but a few seconds later there's a knock at the door—it's open—and Leah and her aunt are standing there. Mom waves them in, and Leah comes up to my bed. "Hey," she says.

"Hey." I wait for her to ask what happened, what kind of idiot goes out on the ice on the night it's all breaking up. But she doesn't.

"I'm glad you're okay." She reaches over to the little table beside my hospital bed and picks up a card. "Did you get this at Forest Hills?" She holds it up. It's the Serenity Prayer.

"Yeah." I look at Mom. "Did you put that there?"

She shakes her head. "The nurse brought it with some loose change and your phone. They had to cut your wet clothes off when they brought you in. Those things must have been in your pocket."

"And the wisdom to know the difference," Leah whispers, and puts the card back. "You know, I wanted to shove that card up Jason's nose when he first gave it to me. But it's true. There's nothing you can do when someone you love is an addict. So you just . . ." She shrugs. "You keep living. And do other stuff."

I look at Leah and remember her on that stage at the Albany feis. "Like dance?"

"Yeah." She smiles and does a few trebles on the hospital's linoleum floor before her aunt says it's time to go. They say good-bye, and then Mom leaves to find me something to drink other than lukewarm water.

I reach over and pick up the card with the Serenity Prayer. I never got to make my last wish when I had the fish. So I make it now. I whisper the words aloud.

"Grant me the serenity to accept the things I cannot change, courage to change the things I can, and the wisdom to know the difference."

I guess it's not a wish exactly. I know the fish is gone.

And that's okay. I'm done talking to fish.

Chapter 23

No Promises

A lot can happen in a week.

A person can win five dance medals and then fall through the ice and end up in the hospital and get released, okay except for a few patches of frostbite.

A person can overdose on heroin, and medicine can just barely save her life, and she can get another chance.

The ice on a whole huge lake can break up, as the wind and waves bite off piece after piece until they're all floating and crashing into each other like ice cubes in a giant's water glass, sparking under the April sun.

And then that first person can take a ferry ride through all those chunks of ice to visit that second person, who's back at a treatment center. Because Sunday is family day with the open AA meeting and brunch.

We pull into the muddy parking lot. A few crocuses are

starting to bloom beside the melting snow banks by the fence now.

Sedgewick runs out of the barn to greet us, and I sigh. When Abby came home before, I was really hoping I'd never see Sedgewick again. But that's not his fault, so I pick a crocus shoot and feed it to him. He likes that even better than Mom's purse.

We go inside and help set up the chairs for the open AA meeting. Abby introduces herself, and everyone says, "Hi, Abby," and then she tells her story. It's the first time I've heard how all this started . . . how she started taking something called Adderall first semester because the college exams are so hard and her friends all told her it would help. But then she couldn't sleep at night, and another friend gave her another pill to fix that. And then after a while, she woke up feeling kind of sick, and the only thing that helped was more of the pills or the light-brown powder she could breathe in, and eventually she injected heroin into her arm with a needle. She was never afraid, she said. Her friends were doing it too. And they were fine. They were fine.

Abby tells everyone at the meeting how she got sicker and sicker until she found help here the first time. She tells them how good it felt to be clean, how happy she was to go home. She takes a deep breath, and her eyes shine with tears. Then she tells them how she was frustrated and lonely, how she took her sister to a dance competition and saw one of her friends from school. Olivia was one of the friends Abby used drugs with. Olivia hadn't been to treatment, but Abby thought she could hang out with her and not do anything, only she couldn't. She thought she was stronger than that, only she wasn't. And so here she is. Again. And she's hurt the people she loves most. Again. And now, Abby looks at us.

"I'm so sorry."

I know that's true. She's sorry. But it's not enough.

So later at brunch, when Mom and Dad are toasting their bagels, I tell her so. And even though I know Abby breaks promises, I want her to make one, the way Mrs. McNeill made me promise not to go on the ice alone. Because maybe it will help her stay clean this time.

So I ask, and Abby shakes her head. No.

"What?" I stare at her. "You left me all alone in Albany so you could run off with your friend, and you can't even make me a stupid promise? Are you planning to just get out of here and do it again?" I try to whisper, but the words spill out faster and louder. "You have to promise or I'm not forgiving you. Promise you'll never use drugs again!"

Abby's eyes shine with tears. She shakes her head. "I am so sorry. I can't."

"Yes, you can! You just won't."

"No. I can't. That's the whole thing with addiction, Charlie. And it's the worst thing in the whole world. Knowing that you want to promise and never, ever hurt the people you love again. And knowing that the addiction is bigger than you, bigger than love, bigger than everything. If I made that promise, I'd be lying. And I'm not going to do that." She takes a deep breath and reaches out for my hand. I pull it back. She folds her hands in her lap, looks at me, and says, "I *do* promise you that I will do everything I can to stay clean. Jason says we have to take it one day at a time. Wake up and say, 'Today, I am not going to use.' And get through that one day. That's what I'm going to do."

I stare at her. Abby used to be so smart and awesome and strong. I hate heroin for making her like this. But I think I believe her. I think she'll try. And I believe she would have promised if she could. "Okay," I say. "I love you. And I get why you can't promise."

"Thank you," Abby says. Then she takes my hand again. I let her, and she holds it hard.

"You should promise, though," Abby says, "because you can. You've never done it. When you've never done it, you can promise never to try. Once you have . . ." She shakes her head, and I see in her eyes how much she wishes she could go back in time, before she ever tried heroin or pills, how much she wishes she could promise. She can't do either of those things now.

But I can.

"Okay," I whisper. "I promise."

And it feels so different from writing my name on that police car, dotting my i with a bubbly orange heart. That's what you don't understand when you take the Sharpie in your hand . . . that addiction is a real thing that can happen. That good people make awful mistakes, and the whole name-signing-on-the-car is just some goofy gimmick that gets you out of math class for the afternoon. It doesn't keep terrible things from happening.

Instead of showing those videos with the greasy-haired people in D.A.R.E. classes, they should show kids like Abby. Soccer forwards and calculus students, student council presidents and homecoming queens and big sisters. They should show those people lying to their families and sitting ashamed in the hospital, tugging on their sleeves to hide the marks on their arms, struggling to breathe, crying when they have to tell the truth. That because they broke a promise they made in fifth grade, nothing can ever be the same.

When brunch is over, we say good-bye to Abby and head home.

Our science fair team agreed to meet at three today, after Drew's drama practice is over. They're having weekend practices because the play's only a week away. Drew's dad finally gave in and let him do that instead of a sport. Drew's playing the part of this funny cowboy, which is more perfect than that drama coach could have known when he saw the lake monster routine and dragged Drew into his club. The only problem is that every time Drew practices lines in front of his nana, she corrects all the *ain't*s to *isn't*s. I really hope she doesn't do that on opening night.

I'm getting out our science fair supplies when Drew shows up, carrying a plate of peanut butter cookies. "Hey, thanks!" I say.

"We made 'em with cricket flour that Nana ordered online."

"Really?" I sniff the cookies. They smell like regular peanut butter cookies, but that's still pretty cool. Our science fair project is almost done. We made a huge poster with pictures of all the different insects that are eaten as food around the world and a graph showing how much protein they have and how environmentally friendly they are to raise, compared to big animals like cows. "These are great. I still wish we'd found a place to order mealworms and fried crickets for tasting at the fair."

"Yeah." Drew stuffs half a cricket-cookie in his mouth. After he swallows it, he asks, "How's your sister doing?"

Earlier this week, I told Catherine and Dasha and Drew what's been happening this winter. I didn't tell them about the fish, because that's too weird to share—who'd believe it? But I told them about Abby and Forest Hills and the real reason I wasn't there to work on the project those other Sundays.

I wish I'd told them sooner. Catherine and Dasha both hugged me and told me they'd be there if my family needed anything at all. Drew told me he was really sorry it all happened. Then he said he'd check his survival guide for tips on getting rid of drug dealers or scarf-eating goats. Catherine punched him on the arm and told him he shouldn't joke about things like this, but what Drew said was okay with me. Making somebody laugh is a pretty good way to be a friend when you're not that into hugging.

"Abby's getting better," I tell him. "She'll be in the treatment center for a few more weeks, and then she says she has to take it one day at a time."

"Cool. I hope she does okay," Drew says. Then he starts singing this peppy "One Day at a Time" song he says is from some old TV show his nana used to watch.

"Nice." I laugh. "I'll share that with Abby next time we go for family day."

Dasha shows up next. Then Catherine arrives with her flour baby strapped in its Snugli carrier over her jacket. Meredith has a new purple hat stretched over her flour-bag head.

"Nice lid," Drew says.

"Thanks!" Catherine pats Meredith. "I knitted it for her."

"When does this project end?" I ask. It feels like Meredith's been around forever.

"I have to turn her in on Thursday," Catherine says. She sounds sad. "I'm going to miss her, in a weird way."

I fill four glasses with milk, and we take everything down to the basement where we've been working.

Before we can really get started, the doorbell rings upstairs, and Mom calls, "Charlie? There's someone here to see you."

I look up, and Bobby O'Sullivan is on his way downstairs with a big box that says ThinkGeek on the side. My heart sinks. I haven't seen Bobby around since I fell through the ice. He's back to sitting with his guy friends from coding club at lunch. I was really hoping that meant that his conjured-up love for me died with the fish, the same way my ice-courage did. But here Bobby is in my basement.

"Hey, Charlie," he says. "I brought you guys something." He sounds less mushy, not so lovesick and smitten. Just normal. He holds out the box, and I look inside.

"You found edible insects?"

"I ordered them a few weeks ago when you first mentioned the project. I guess . . ." He looks confused about why he ordered bugs for someone else's science project. He does not look even the tiniest bit in love with me. "I guess I thought you could use help. I'm not sure."

"Well, thanks! We'll totally pay you back for them." The box is full of little tins—all labeled. "You guys! We are so having an insect tasting at this science fair! We have bacon and cheese grasshoppers, barbecue bamboo worms, salted queen weaver ants, armor tail scorpions with seaweed, and wasabi crickets!"

"Be careful," Bobby says, clearing his throat. "I sampled those. They're *very* spicy."

"That's okay. Thanks for doing this," I say. And then, because I still feel bad about wishing him in love with me, I add, "Um . . . are you already working on a project with someone? Because if you're not, you can help with ours. If you want." I wait to see if he's going to go all gaga on me again, but he's looking across the room at Dasha, who's taken out her phone.

"Is that Pong?" he asks. "Did you write the code for it?"

Her face lights up, and she nods.

He looks back at me. "Yeah, that'd be cool, I guess." Then he leaves me holding the bug box and rushes over to Dasha. "Dude! That is awesome. How'd you debug it so the ball bounces right in the corners?" They geek out over the bouncing electronic dot, while the rest of us polish off the cookies and finish up our presentation until it's time to leave for dance.

Drew and Bobby say good-bye. Dasha and Catherine have their stuff all ready, so they wait while I change and load up my dance bag. Tonight's the first Novice class for Dasha and me.

"Are you nervous?" I ask her on the way in. Catherine hurries ahead to get Meredith set up in her chair. This is the last dance class she'll get to watch.

"I'm a little scared." Dasha does a few dance steps in the hallway. "But we're ready, don't you think?"

"More than ready!" I fall in step with her. Our rain boots thump quietly, but it's still fun.

"Hard shoes first today, ladies and gentlemen!" Miss Brigid calls from the studio. She sees us and smiles. "You ready to work?"

"Absolutely!"

Dasha and I lace our shoes and head into the studio. I take a deep breath. It's funny the way stale school-basement air can make a person feel so alive. But to me, this isn't the smell of old pencils and textbooks. It's the smell of dancing, the smell of hard work and loud stomps and joy.

"Let's start with the hornpipe!" Miss Brigid calls over the music.

Catherine waves at me in the mirror as the music starts. I smile and take a deep breath. When the beat hits, I lift my knee and kick out.

And I'm dancing. Dancing and stomping and kicking, and the loudness of these fast, stomping shoes fills the room. It fills me, until I'm out of breath but bursting with energy because even when I'm scared and worried about Abby, this . . . this is something I can do. I can fill myself with the energy of this dance, the sound of music and stomps and clicks, the feeling of flying over the floor with Dasha beside me.

It feels amazing. It's enough. And I'm not wishing for anything else.

Author's Note

This was a scary book for me to research and to write, because the truth is that addiction is a disease that can strike any family at any time, with devastating results. Heroin use, in particular, has been steadily increasing in the United States. According to the Centers for Disease Control and Prevention, heroin use among young adults ages eighteen to twenty-five more than doubled from 2002 to 2013. In those same years, the rate of heroin-related deaths almost quadrupled.

Heroin is an opiate drug that is highly addictive. The drug has chemicals that bind to receptors in a user's brain. This can lead quickly to both physical and mental addiction that makes people seek the drug at the expense of everything else in their lives. Heroin use is linked not only to fatal overdoses but also to HIV, hepatitis, liver and kidney disease, digestive problems, collapsed veins, crime, and violence.

Treatments are available for heroin addiction. Most of these focus on getting the addict through painful withdrawal symptoms and helping to restore the person's normal brain function while forming healthier habits. This involves breaking ties with friends who use illegal drugs and avoiding places where drugs were used in the past.

Here are some places where you can learn more about addiction and families and how to find help:

The National Council on Alcoholism and Drug Dependence has a web page dedicated to providing information for families (https://ncadd.org/for-friends-and-family/family-disease-and-recovery).

Alcoholics Anonymous, the group Abby attends at her treatment center, is a support group for alcoholics as well as people addicted to other drugs (http://www.aa.org/).

Al-Anon and Alateen are groups that offer support and understanding for families of alcoholics and addicts (http://www.al-anon.org/).

I'd like to extend my sincerest thanks to the people who shared information and personal stories with me as I researched this book. Michaela von Elbe, you are a phenomenal, strong woman, and I'm so thankful you chose to share your story with me. I'm also grateful to Tara Cota of

Maple Leaf Treatment Center in Underhill, Vermont, who answered my many questions about heroin addiction and treatment.

I'm appreciative of the small village of experts who helped with this novel. Art LaGrange shared his ice fishing experiences on Lake Champlain and showed me how to use an auger. Teachers Eliza Coyle and Lisa Berner talked with me about their work with ESL students. Emily Hambly and her mom, Carolyn, answered my questions about wigs and Irish dance dresses at a feis in Syracuse. Michelle Germain gave me a wonderful tutorial on all things Irish dance, while Wendy Watts Scalfaro, Jackie Germain, and Diane and Khila Pecoraro helped with last-minute questions. Thanks also to Champlain Valley Irish Dance and Marie Short for allowing me to sit in on classes with my notebook. It was a wonderfully loud and joyful place to brainstorm.

I'm grateful to the warm community of writer and reader friends who encouraged, critiqued, nudged, and shared lattes with me. Many thanks to early readers Linda Urban, Loree Griffin Burns, Liza Martz, Eric Luper, Ella Messner, and Meghan and Michelle Germain.

If I could, I'd send a bouquet of ice flowers to the whole amazing Bloomsbury team, especially my editor, Mary Kate Castellani, who remained calm and supportive when I told her I was writing a magical-ice-fishing-Irish-dancing-heroin novel for kids. Thanks to my agent, Jennifer Laughran, for being a smart, fierce advocate as well as a friend. Most of all, thanks to all the Schirmers, Messners, Rupperts, and Alois, especially Tom, Jake, and Ella. Even if I caught a magic fish, I couldn't wish for a more wonderful family.